APRIL IN PARIS

Michael Wallner

Translated from the German by
John Cullen

WINDSOR
PARAGON

First published 2007
by
John Murray (Publishers)
This Large Print edition published 2007
by
BBC Audiobooks Ltd by arrangement with
John Murray (Publishers)
A division of Hodder Headline

Hardcover ISBN: 978 1 405 61794 9
Softcover   ISBN: 978 1 405 61795 6

Text © Michael Wallner 2006
Translation © John Cullen 2007

British Library Cataloguing in Publication Data available

Printed and bound in Great Britain by
Antony Rowe Ltd., Chippenham, Wiltshire

APRIL IN PARIS

When people on Paris's bustling streets look at Michael Roth, they see little more than a Parisian student. What they do not realize is that he is carrying a painful secret, one that he cannot even reveal to the woman he loves.

For Michael is no ordinary Frenchman but a German soldier. He has been sent to Paris to assist the Nazis in dealing with Resistance fighters. Desperate to escape his daily life, he steals into the world of the oppressed Parisians, and into the path of Chantal. But as Michael falls for the bookseller's beautiful daughter, he discovers that a person's past always catches up with them. Soon he will be forced to make the ultimate sacrifice and choose between his country, his life and his destiny.

For John and Martha Wallner

PONT ROYAL, 1943

1

I learned about the transfer before noon. The small stripes of light had reached the windowsill. My major came in and kept one hand on the doorknob while gesturing to me with the other to keep my seat. He wanted to know if the hogwash from Marseille was ready yet. I pointed to the half-written sheet still in the typewriter. I could go when I reached the end of the page, he said.

'And the dispatch from Lagny-sur-Marne?' I asked, surprised.

'Someone else will have to do it. You're needed elsewhere.'

I pressed my knees together under the table. In those days, many people were being sent to the front.

'I'm being reassigned?'

'Rue des Saussaies has lost a translator.' The major ran his hand down the left side of his uniform coat. German Horseman's Badge, War Merit Cross. He said he'd do all he could to get me back. I shouldn't worry, he said; my transfer would be only temporary.

'What happened to the translator from rue des Saussaies?'

'He was run over and killed last night.'

I flinched. 'Partisans?'

'Of course not. The guy was drunk, and he went staggering over a bridge. Because of the blackout, the patrol car saw him too late. Unfortunately, he didn't die right away. Horrible. Anyway, the request for an interpreter wound up on my desk.

3

You seem to have a *reputation* in rue des Saussaies,' the major said with a rare smile. 'They specifically asked for *you.*'

My back stiffened. I glanced across the room toward the wall map, scale 1:500,000. Arrows, hatching, the plaster rosette over the door, the remains of cloth wallpaper from the time when people still *lived* here. My desk, the French dictionary, badly chewed pencils. I was going to miss the lovely view out over the line of roofs to the west.

The major looked at me gloomily. 'Finish the Marseille thing. Then take the rest of the day off. You start over there tomorrow morning. You'll be back in a few days. Those folks aren't particularly fond of strange faces.'

I stood up and saluted; the major absentmindedly raised his arm. I remained standing even after he left the room. The sunlight came through the window and cast a shadow like a cross on the wall. All at once, I was cold. I buttoned my top button and grabbed my cap, as though I was about to leave. Then I put it down again, lowered myself onto the chair, read the French original, and began typing the translation with two fingers.

You could have gone another way, I said to myself. How careless, to walk down rue des Saussaies, of all streets. The black-and-silver uniform appeared quite suddenly, right in front of SS headquarters. A brief exchange of words. Did he ask for a light? You'd better be careful. Only translate expressions from the dictionary. Stare at the table. Never look anyone in the face. Forget whatever they let you see. In the evening, you'll go

4

to your hotel; in the morning, you'll report for duty on time. Until they don't need you anymore. Then you'll go back to your major, who doesn't want to do anything but enjoy the city and relish the role of the conqueror and leaves it to you to push arrows and numbers around and adorns your reports with his name. As long as you remain indispensable, he'll keep them from sending you into the real war.

*   *   *

The Pont Royal was standing in water up to its shoulders, only half a metre shy of the high-water mark set in 1700 and something. Fishermen leaned over the parapet wall. The stones were already warm, and people were sitting around with half-closed eyes, facing the sun. When they heard the hobnailed boots approaching, some turned away. I plunged into the hubbub of the Latin Quarter. The more people there were, the less conspicuously foreign I was. The waters of the Seine raged in the steel framework of the Pont Solférino. A stout Oriental woman at a produce stand picked up three miserable apples and felt them, one after another. Not far away, a private first class and his comrade stood gawking at her. A silver half-moon glistened on her forehead.

'Great-looking women they've got here,' said the private first class.

The other nodded. 'I'd be willing to sully the Aryan race with a bit of that.'

Despite her corpulence, she was elegant, but she behaved as though she had no right to be on the street. When the owner of the shop came out and glared at her suspiciously, she put the apples back. After a few uncertain steps, she noticed the soldiers, who were standing in her way with grins fixed on their faces.

I stepped behind the field grey uniforms and ducked into a narrow side street. I was walking uncomfortably fast, setting a blistering pace, in fact, when what I actually wanted to do was stroll. I counted the hotel signs as they glided past overhead. Go into one, I thought, ask for a room on the top floor. Take off your boots—easy does it—open the floor-to-ceiling window, and let time slip motionlessly by.

I slowed my pace. The shop across the street was several rooms deep. Back in the farthest room, a lightbulb was burning. I crossed the street. In front of the entrance, there was a stack of chairs with pink coverings. I bent down and touched the splitting silk. Someone in the rear of the shop raised his head. The light made his face stand out sharply against the shadowy background. When he looked at me, I straightened up quickly, as if I'd been caught doing something forbidden.

I looked for wider streets, more people, more of a crush. Most of the shops were already closed, empty behind reddish brown metal bars, offering nothing to the hurrying passersby. A bakery was still open, though the line was long. I joined it, avoiding people's eyes. They kept their distance from the uniform. I bought a loaf of flour-sprinkled bread. As I stepped out, a garçon was sweeping up wood shavings from the sidewalk.

I passed a black gate I'd seen before without ever noticing that it led not into a building but into a narrow street, practically an alley. I drew myself

6

up to decipher the faded street sign. Rue de Gaspard? The gate was shut. Although I was curious, I hesitated. Then I leaned on the gate, and one of its panels gave way. Passing pedestrians scrutinized me as I stood there like that, half in the street, half in the entrance. I looked past the iron threshold. The little street disappeared in the shadow of a wall. Gray light on the pavement. I slipped through the gate and set off down the alley. Closed shutters everywhere. Where the buildings werc lowest, the evening sun shone through.

When I turned the corner, I came upon a junk dealer who was carrying his wares back into his shop. With a bronze bust in his arms, he blocked my way, unintimidated by my uniform. I noticed a pendulum clock lcaning against the wall. Walnut housing, polished brass pendulum.

I said, *'Il me semble que j'ai vu exactement la même à Munich.'*

My unaccented French surprised him. *'C'est possible, monsieur. Je l'ai achetée d'une famille qui a vécu longtemps en Allemagne.'*

'Quel est votre prix?'

The dealer named a price for the clock, a sum no Frenchman would consider paying. I offered half as much. He wouldn't yield so much as a centime, claiming he'd promised not to sell the clock for less than it was worth.

I said, 'Well then, I'm sorry,' and penetrated farther into rue de Gaspard.

A young woman was sitting motionless on a stone that lay like a rock fallen from the sky in front of a bookshop. I could make out her slender legs under her coat. She was reading. When I was

7

nearly past her, she looked up. I went no farther and stepped into the shop instead. The man behind the counter had grey hair, combed with a part. He was holding the stump of an unlighted cigar in his mouth and spreading paste on paper labels with a stringy brush. He took a quick glance at my uniform.

'*Vous cherchez quelque chose de spécial?*' he muttered without interest. Indifferent to my reply, he stuck a little label onto a book's spine. I indicated that I'd take a look around. The gesture he made in response was more dismissive than inviting. I stepped over to the shelves next to the window. My finger glided over the backs of the books as I looked out through the dull glass.

She was still sitting on the stone. A uniquely beautiful face. Outsized eyes, a seductively round forehead under reddish brown curls. Her face had a cunning, feline look and softly curving lips; her chin was too short and ran sharply back to her throat.

A butterfly lighted on the windowsill. The girl jerked her head up as though someone had bumped into her. Slowly, she laid the book aside, stood up, and walked over to the window, where the butterfly remained with trembling wings. As she approached, I withdrew between the bookshelves, step by step. She reached the low window on tiptoe, her eyes fixed on the butterfly. When she was only a few metres away, she stared in my direction—and didn't notice me.

With several books in my hands, I was suddenly conscious of the shop owner's scrutiny. He closed up the pot of glue and stepped forward. '*Vous avez trouvé?*' he asked.

I turned around, and so I didn't see if the butterfly flew away. The man was a head shorter than me; his balding scalp gleamed through his parted hair.

I took a step toward the exit. *'Il y en a trop. Je ne sais pas comment choisir.'*

With that, I laid the books down, reached the open door, and crossed threshold and step in one stride. My boot struck the pavement hard.

She was gone. My eyes searched behind some bushes and then shifted to the gate at the end of the little street. Her book lay on the stone. I gazed at the slim volume without touching it. *Le Zéro*; the title meant nothing to me. Suddenly, as I looked up at all the shuttered windows, I felt that someone was watching me from behind them. Slowly, but covering a lot of ground with each step, I made for the black entrance gate and passed through to the street outside, avoiding two sullen-looking French cops on patrol. I turned into the tree-lined avenue.

2

Where have you been?' the SS corporal asked. I hadn't slept well, I was nervous, and I'd been waiting for two hours. I'd tried to find a comfortable position on the bench in the hall. An unbroken stream of officers came and went, and I kept having to snap to attention. My military pay book and papers had been checked on the ground floor. Only after a telephone call had the guards let me through. On the way up, I'd admired the green-veined marble stairs. Diplomats and their ladies had strolled up and down these steps in days gone by. You could almost forget where you were.

'Where were you?' the SS corporal repeated.

'Out here. Where else?' I replied without standing up. We were equal in rank, this fellow and I. The first day in a new posting determines how you're going to be treated there.

'You'd better lose that tone of voice.' He directed me to follow him. 'Do you know shorthand?' he asked over his shoulder.

A simple yes would have sufficed. I said, 'If I didn't, I probably wouldn't be here.'

'Is that so?' The SS corporal turned around and grinned unpleasantly. 'We've got a lot of people in this place who don't know a thing about stenography.'

I clamped my jaws together and walked on in silence. I was twenty-two, and I hadn't yet been to the front. But I'd become a soldier at an age when it couldn't be avoided forever. I was one of two brothers. My father didn't have the money to send us both to university, but Otto had been allowed to study medicine. I'd begun a law course, just to show that I could get by without the family's help; however, the war had relieved me of making any further decisions.

We entered the offices of the unit I'd been assigned to. Tall oaken doors, a powerful-looking woman in civilian clothes, two soldiers sitting at typewriters. I had to wait some more. Finally, the SS corporal knocked on the first office door. I went in and stood across from the thin man I'd met three days before, when I was walking down rue des Saussaies.

'Ah, it's you,' he said, looking up from his papers. 'Have you been told what you have to do?'

'Not in detail.' I was standing stiffly erect, even though the regulations didn't require me to.

'Details are important.' He took up the greenish grey file and got to his feet. Average height, and slighter than I remembered, despite the tight-fitting uniform. Head almost bald, mouth strikingly sorrowful.

'This way,' he said. He opened the barrier beside his desk and the double door behind it. Before stepping through the door, he asked, 'Roth, am I right?'

'Corporal Roth, yes, sir,' I replied.

'How long in the army?'

'Since March 1940, Captain.'

'You picked the best time.'

I didn't know whether the reference was to our victorious campaign or my new duty assignment. We came into a brightly lighted room.

The first thing I saw was the boy's face, his wet hair hanging down over his forehead. In the corner stood a tub of water, the water still moving. He was a kid, fifteen at most, with his hands tied behind his back. I could smell his fear. I noticed two uniforms, both SS corporals, and I produced my writing pad. The captain took a seat and made a brusque gesture toward a smaller table. My pencil fell to the floor. I picked it up as unobtrusively as I could, took the few steps to the table, and cast my eyes down. Everything started immediately, without any transition.

3

I hurried back to the hotel and fell onto the bed
that nearly filled up my room. From the floor
above my head came the sounds of rushing water
and boots flung into a corner: Hirschbiegel, the
bather, had come home. This could go on for
hours. I laid the loaf of bread on the table, but I
couldn't eat anything. I stared at the faded
shepherdesses on the wall and tried not to pay
attention to the noise. The beds were placed head-
to-head on either side of the wall, which was as
thin as cardboard. Someone on the telephone next
door said, 'So what's up? . . . I have no idea. The
best place is where we were the day before
yesterday. Jardin something or other. Oh, and I'm
bringing someone with me . . . You know very
well.'

Another noise source: the elevator. Luftwaffe
meeting on the fifth floor; the soldier manning the
lift was ferrying air force officers up and down. I
stood uncertainly between the bed and the table,
aware of my heartbeat, as I had frequently been in
recent weeks. I turned to the mirror. The narrow
nose, the dark eyebrows. They made me think
about earlier photographs. It wasn't my mouth that
had become harder; it was my eyes. You need a
haircut, I thought, wetting my fingers and
smoothing the hair on the side of my head. I slowly
sank back onto the bed. I was thirsty, but there was
nothing left to drink in the room. My eyes fell on
my boots. I didn't want to go out dressed like *that*,
not this evening.

I sat there for several long minutes, my head on my chest and my shoulders sagging. The people I'd seen on the Pont Royal had been lounging on the sun-warmed stones, their eyes shut and turned toward the light. Should someone wearing military boots pass by, they'd open their eyes. I feared those moments, when they turned away or withdrew into their homes, when they murmured curses I heard and understood. If I didn't have to look different from them, I was someone who could blend in anywhere, in any city. I wanted to disappear among them, to be part of them; no one had a right to see the *other* in me. Since the glorious days when we marched into Paris, I'd felt nothing but anxiety.

Slowly, like a man reaching a difficult decision, I got up and opened the wardrobe. How long had it been since I'd worn the suit with the little checks? I discovered a moth hole, luckily in an inconspicuous spot. I took the suit off the hanger and held the coat in front of my chest.

'You could be an office worker,' I said to the mirror. 'Or a waiter whose shift is over. Maybe you work in a bookshop. You paste little labels onto book covers and run errands.' I glanced at my shelves—half the books were French. I'll put one of them under my arm, I thought, and go where lots of people stroll about. There would be less danger that way.

I got the dry sausage and an apple from the drawer. The bread crumbled when I broke it. I sliced the sausage with my clasp knife and ate slowly. Had the boy they were interrogating really stolen the carburetors? He'd merely been seen in the area. Five buses for prisoner transport, and not

13

one of them would start; the carburetors were missing. I observed my hands as I cut the sausage. The boy's blood had dried on his skin. I stopped chewing. A sudden realization: In civilian clothes, you won't get out of the hotel. I listened to my heartbeat. If rue des Saussaies learns about this, I thought, your ass is cooked.

I wiped my mouth on the towel, stood up, reached into the wardrobe, and took out the cloth bag I usually used to carry my laundry. In the room above mine, Hirschbiegel began to play music. 'Ma Pomme.' I buttoned up my uniform and pulled on my boots.

I met a Luftwaffe lieutenant and his female companion on the stairs. I came to attention; he looked past me.

'Dans quelques minutes, j'ai temps pour toi,' the lieutenant said, awkwardly stringing the words together.

'Pour faire quoi?' the woman asked with a laugh.

At the reception desk, the sentry was talking to the toilet attendant, a young woman who spoke a few words of German. The sentry offered her some sweets. The chocolate bars were stuck together, and he grinned; her eyes remained serious. I walked down the hall, carrying my bag. The walls were painted dark brown, with scratches and scrapes from passing luggage. It was a corridor I walked through every day, but this time the exit seemed farther away with each step.

'Hey, soldier!'

I kept walking.

'Just a second, you!'

I turned my head, as though he couldn't possibly be speaking to me.

'Hirschbiegel was asking for you!' the sentry called out.

'When?'

'He said he knocked on your door and you weren't there.'

Through the glass, I saw a Luftwaffe major approaching the entrance.

'Thanks,' I called over my shoulder, got through the door in three steps, held it open for the major, and stood ramrod-straight until he reached the reception desk. The toilet attendant disappeared into her niche.

I hurried through the streets, as though I had some particular place to go. In spite of the sun, a cold east wind was blowing, stirring up dust as it passed. Golden seeds were stuck in horse manure. Scraps of paper circled in the air. To get my excitement under control, I murmured the names of the streets. When I passed a damaged building slated for demolition, I slowed down and looked around. A first glance made me think the place had taken a direct hit. Part of the facade hung over the sidewalk, and the support beams were ready to give way at any moment. I stepped into the entry-way. Burst water pipes gaped in the remains of the walls. I listened, wiped dust off a ledge, and laid out my suit. It was an awkward process, getting out of my boots in a standing position; I hopped around and made more noise than I liked. Then I stuffed my uniform coat and trousers into the bag. For a few seconds, I stood in my underwear in the empty corridor. Steps from outside scared me, and I tried to take refuge in the collapsed stairwell. But whoever it was walked on by. Not daring to take off my ID tags, I just threw them over my shoulder

15

so that they hung down my back, and then I quickly slipped on my shirt and pants and tied my shoes. My boots bulged in the laundry bag; I would have been conspicuous, carrying something like that. I investigated the entrance hall. The stairway curved up into a blind spot where no light fell. I addressed a quick prayer to the heavens and shoved the bag into the darkness. I was about to put on my soft felt hat when, at the last moment, I spotted the label—Klawischnigg & Söhne, München. I bit the thread off, ripped out the little strip of cloth, and threw it away. I pulled the hat down low over my forehead.

I walked out into the street as *another.* I'd laid aside all my privileges; I was defenceless against both occupiers and occupied. I must not show my papers or speak my language. *One* false word would betray me. And by 7:30 at the latest, I had to metamorphose back into my former self. All the same, I didn't take my watch, an heirloom engraved with a German inscription.

The first thing I wanted was a new name, and before I could figure out why and wherefore, I opted for Antoine. Monsieur Antoine, assistant bookseller. I took the small volume out of my pocket: La Fontaine's *Fables.* The book gave me security; it reinforced my biography. Monsieur Antoine, out for a stroll. Only a low-profile promenader, a young man in a check-patterned suit. His footfall sounded the same as that of the people around him. No heavy stepping, no reason for anyone to clear out of his way. I gradually returned to normal breathing and loosened my fearful grip on La Fontaine. I pushed my hat up high on my forehead. For no good reason, I smiled

16

into the late afternoon.

Monsieur Antoine crossed the Pont Royal and turned into the commercial streets near the quays. Fruit and vegetable stands appeared. Beside them, people were drinking red wine from little glasses. I turned the corner and was immediately surrounded by a babble of voices. Everyone spoke! I heard old men laughing after a girl with a flowered hat passed them. A fat woman shouted across the street, and three other women answered. An abbé, his shoulders gleaming in the bronze-coloured light, blinked at a matron and made arcane predictions about the weather. The noisy, chattering world seized me and carried me away into the sounds and the voices. I stopped in front of an old woman with an accordion and tossed a coin into her dish.

'*Que désirez-vous, mon garçon?*' she asked, taking the pipe out of her mouth.

I had resolved to speak as little as possible. Monsieur Antoine, however, found this notion mistaken. On a spring afternoon, a *silent* Parisian would be conspicuous. Everyone around was bustling, boisterous, and abrupt.

There was a song I wanted to hear, a hit, but all I could think of was the refrain: '*Je te veux.*' The old woman nodded appreciatively, stuck the pipe into the corner of her mouth, and began. I listened to her for a while and then walked on. I noticed a lady, a *madame*, wearing a veil as thin as gossamer; her mouth was painted dark red. A band of teenagers ran past while a cop ambled away in the opposite direction.

I got in line in front of a pastry shop. A small woman crowded me from behind. On the other

17

side of the counter, a skinny shop assistant was tying up packages of cookies. I watched an apprentice, a young girl, furrowing her brow as she read a cheap novel, oblivious to the entire world. I would have been only too happy to know what she found in those words. I got the last remaining package of cookies and paid for it; the small woman gave me dirty looks. I thought about giving her the cookies, but then I laid my book on the package and stuck them both under my arm.

While loitering in front of the shop windows, assuring myself that my suit could pass for a French model, I realized that I had turned into rue de Gaspard.

Today, the narrow street gleamed with a different light. The sinking sun lay deep in the sky, bathing ridges and roofs in warm red. There was no one on the stone in front of the bookshop. I figured it would be senseless to search for the young woman with the cat's face. She'd probably just happened to be there that one time, bought a book, sat on the stone, and read for a while. Then she had gone away, and there was a good chance she'd never return to rue de Gaspard.

The bookshop was closed. Disappointed, I looked up at the name over the portal: JOFFO, LIVRES. Out of curiosity, I tried the door handle. The door opened, and the shop bell rang.

I said in French, 'May I come in?'

'Please do, monsieur. Have a look around,' the owner replied from behind the counter.

I went to a shelf and stood in such a way that he could see my face. I asked him, 'Do you have the new translation of *Anna Karenina*?'

'There's no new translation.' The corpulent

gentleman shook his head and came closer to me. 'At the moment, there's nothing of the sort being published. Prospère has shut down.'

Looking the bookseller right in the eyes, I asked to see the old edition. Would he recognize the German corporal who had visited his shop only yesterday?

'This is from before the war,' I remarked.

'As I said.' He shrugged his shoulders and then noticed the little volume under my arm. 'You're reading the *Fables*?' He reached out a hand. 'May I?'

I gave him my favorite book.

'This is a rare edition.' He smiled the smile of a connoisseur.

Fear came over me. Maybe the book bore a German mark of some kind.

Joffo turned to the copyright page. 'Look here. This must be the last printing: 1936.' He looked at me. 'Are you perhaps interested in selling this book?'

'Unfortunately, I can't.' I sighed, much relieved. 'It was a gift.'

'I know I must still have . . .' Much more agile than his bulk suggested, the man dashed over to the next set of shelves and pulled out the fabulous, sumptuously illustrated edition. He showed me the poem called 'Fortune and the Young Boy'; the illustration was a full-page engraving by Gustave Doré.

'I used to read from this book to my daughter when she was little,' Joffo said.

On the margin of the page, I noticed words scribbled in a childish hand. Suddenly, I seemed to see the butterfly girl, the young woman with the reddish brown hair. My idea was crazy, but I gave it a try. 'I haven't seen your daughter at all today.'

His head jerked up. His eyes narrowed like a boar's. He said, 'Have we met, monsieur?'

'No,' I replied with a smile. 'But I'm in the neighbourhood now and again.'

'And your name?'

'Antoine...' My eyes quickly searched book spines. Strings of letters, gold embossing, a curved *r* and *e,* and over there an anthology entitled *Les Barbares.* 'Antoine Rebarbes,' I said. I took a deep breath.

'You're from Paris?'

'From outside of Paris,' I said as calmly as possible. 'Will you wrap up the Tolstoy for me?'

He hesitated before going behind the counter and wrapping *Anna Karenina* in brown paper. I pulled a banknote out of my pocket.

'Oh? They're printing these again?' Joffo held the new bill against the light. My money came from the offices of the Wehrmacht.

'I was wondering that myself.'

'About time,' he said, turning the bill over and over. 'The old ones fall apart in your fingers.'

The banknote disappeared into the cash drawer. He counted out the change. 'Where did you meet my daughter?' he asked craftily. 'In the salon, perhaps?'

I hesitated. What kind of *salon* would I be likely to meet her in? I said, 'Right, in the salon.' I took my coins and turned to go.

The suspicious Joffo came after me. 'You're in the neighbourhood only now and then, and you get your hair cut here?'

I tried to guess the connection as I opened the

door. 'Why not? He's an excellent barber.' I smiled and stepped outside.

Joffo held on to the door so the bell wouldn't ring twice.

'Good evening, monsieur,' I said over my shoulder. I felt his eyes on me as I walked away. The key was turning in the lock. I started on my way back through the narrow street.

'How much for the pendulum clock?' I asked the junk dealer.

He named half the price from the last time.

I stepped out onto the boulevard.

4

I was hot. My jacket was slung over my shoulder, and I had my hat pushed back on my head. For the past hour, I'd been looking for a *salon de coiffure*. Children were climbing noisily over garbage cans in rue Jacob. I came to a stop. There was no sign over the entrance and only a little light inside. As I looked more closely, however, I could see two bottom-heavy chairs, some bottles on a shelf, and in front of the shelf a man of average height with a pair of scissors in his hand. On the right, customers sat waiting. I walked on. After a few steps, I turned back. I entered the shop and looked around; no sign of the cat girl.

'You won't have long to wait, monsieur.' The boss was hardly older than I was. He was wearing a close-fitting jacket that buttoned up the side. 'There's just this gentleman ahead of you.'

Two customers were on their feet, paying, and

blocking my view of a third. The two left the shop.

I saw the leather belt, the black cap on a knee, the silver death's head. An SS major. His boot heels clicked together when he stood up. The barber gestured to his chair, inviting the officer to sit down. Just as I was about to slip out, he looked at me. I dropped onto a seat next to an old man with a newspaper.

'Would monsieur like a nice short haircut?' the barber asked, throwing a towel across the major's shoulders as soon as he settled into the chair.

The officer looked at himself in the mirror without interest. He understood nothing and pointed to the side where he wanted the part. The barber sprayed water on the back of his neck.

My eyes fell on the holster. The metal plate was shiny, as though it were a toy pistol. Passersby outside stopped to watch as the barber drew his comb through the SS officer's hair.

The scissors clicked. The barber's fingers moved rapidly up and down the back of the officer's head. Smooth, supple hands, browned by the sun. I crossed my arms.

During the interrogation, the boy's fingers had stuck out from his hands like spokes from a broken wheel, motionless, stiff—as though they no longer belonged to him. He didn't cry out while they were dislocating his fingers; it was only later that he wept. I forced myself to think about other hands. The hands of the man fishing on the Pont Royal: one laid flat on the parapet, the other clutching the rod with great tenderness. Only the fingertips had pulled at the line, furtively, as if the fisherman himself were not supposed to notice this manipulation. The SS officer had big freckled

22

hands. They lay calmly in his lap. Clip-clip, over the nape of his neck and the back of his head.

The door opened. A mother was dragging her son to get a haircut. She saw the officer and stopped short.

'Oh, oh,' she said. 'In that case, I'll look in later.' Then she disappeared, pulling her baffled son behind her.

Against the barber's will, the major turned his head and observed the children playing noisily outside the door. 'Yours?' he wanted to know.

'No, monsieur.' The barber carefully turned the officer's head back to the proper position.

'Whose are they?' the major asked in awkward French.

'They're my brothers,' said a woman's voice.

Holding a broom in one hand, she stepped through a beaded curtain. She looked more substantial in her white coat, definitely older than twenty. Her hair framed her head in ringlets and curls. Her large eyes looked serious. Joy warmed my belly as I involuntarily leaned forward. The clip-clipping stopped.

'Pretty kids.' The lieutenant nodded. He added in German, 'War's hardest on children.'

She laid the broom aside and went to the door. She wasn't wearing any stockings, and I stared at her calves. As the shop bell rang, she called the boys by name. They broke off their game. Flushed faces, momentary paralysis. Then they understood the warning, went to the end of the street, and disappeared.

With a flick of his wrist, the barber snatched away the towel and held up a mirror so the major could see the results of his work. The officer nodded, expressionless, and stood up. About to lay the gold coin on the shop counter, he turned around and put the piece in the young woman's hand instead. Stone-faced, she opened the till and dropped the coin inside.

'I'm looking for a restaurant,' he said to no one in particular. 'The Peletier.'

The barber shook his head. The woman with the reddish brown hair didn't answer, either.

I pressed my fingers against my palms, stood up, and stepped in front of the major. Did I do it to impress her? Did I want to put my own disguise to the test? I'd heard of the Peletier. The SS ordered up women there. 'It's behind Saint-Germain-des-Prés, on the south side of the square,' I said. We looked each other in the eyes. 'You can't miss it.'

'*Merci, monsieur,*' the major said, using the hard German *s* and putting on his cap. While his boots were still crunching over the threshold, I took my seat in the barber's chair. The young woman swept up the German officer's hair.

'Why did you say they were your *brothers*?' the barber said to the young woman as the major was vanishing among the crowds in the street. 'Don't play games with these people, Chantal!'

'They're Samuel's kids.' She was sweeping quite close to me.

The barber spread a fresh towel over my shoulders. I watched the young woman in the mirror.

'How come you know the Peletier?' she asked when our eyes met. 'Only pigs go there.'

'Chantal!' The barber looked around. The old man behind the newspaper didn't move.

'In that case, I gave him the right directions.' I

24

smiled. 'Trim the back and sides, please.'

'We haven't had the honour of serving you before, monsieur,' the barber said.

What struck me about his delicate face was its long nose—as though it had been set there maliciously. 'I'm here on a visit,' I said.

'Travelling is complicated at the moment,' he remarked insinuatingly.

I nodded. 'It took me two days. God knows how many times we stopped. The track's closed between Thiers and Moulins.'

I was amazed at how effortlessly my brain spat out lies. I focused mentally on an image of the Ordnance Survey map. Armed bands, enemy units, arrows and hatching, the front approximately garter-high. The barber moistened the hair on the back of my head. The scissors approached my temple. I shut my eyes. The place grew quiet. From time to time, the old man turned a page. The woman named Chantal was now sitting behind the till. The bookshop owner's daughter, I thought, trying to imagine her growing up among thousands of books. In the evenings, her father would take down the *Fables* and read some of them to her. After Chantal herself learned to read, on fine days she would carry her books outside, sit on the stone, and immerse herself in them . . . The sound of the scissors made me sleepy. As though from a great distance, I saw Antoine sitting in the barber's chair. Moments before, he'd aroused suspicion by giving directions to an SS man. He was also suspect because he came from out of town. Denunciations were more and more frequent; collaborators and informers were everywhere. The French didn't even trust one another. Monsieur

25

Antoine couldn't speak to Chantal, neither in the shop nor on the street. For a German, on the other hand, meeting women was easy in those days. Women in German company were exempt from curfew rules, and the bars were full. Parisian women fed their families by going out with German officers. I opened my eyes and watched Chantal in the mirror.

The barber finished his job, and I stood up. She brushed me off. While I was paying, she didn't deign to look at me. No one held the door open for me. Both of them were silent until I left the shop. Through the window, I could see them start talking as soon as I was outside.

My freshly cut hair made me itch. I put my hat on, thinking about taking a seat in the café on the other side of the square and waiting for Chantal to get off work. A ridiculous idea. I sauntered up rue Bonaparte to the quay. The river still looked swollen and angry. A Wehrmacht staff sergeant leaned over the parapet and told his companion that the water level was falling. The fishermen had gone home. Not for the first time, I spotted one of the little *V*'s. The Parisians made the *V* for Victory sign everywhere. Folded subway tickets, broken matches. Someone had made a V-shaped tear in a newspaper; a gust of wind blew the page in front of me.

I was already past the Eiffel Tower when I heard the ringing. It made me jump. Which church? What time was it? A second bell joined in. I started counting the strokes; at six, I turned around. When the bell struck a seventh time, I began to run along the quai d'Orsay, but not unreasonably fast. When field grey uniforms appeared, I slowed my pace. A patrol passed. I stopped under a plane tree and waited for my breathing to calm down. Then I crossed the Pont Royal, reached the neighbourhood where my hotel was, and turned into the narrow alley I thought I'd made a mental note of. The streets were starting to empty out around me. Women with string shopping bags hurried by. Some sauntering young men pretended to be taking a leisurely stroll, but they knew they didn't dare get caught outside after eight o'clock.

Hard as I tried, I couldn't find the ruined building with the passageway again! Now I was running, looking up at the roofs of the buildings, hoping to spot a landmark. When, after yet another vain search, I found myself in front of a tailor shop for the third time, I saw in there the only possibility of getting back to my hotel.

'Are you coming with us to Turachevsky's later?' A group of air force officers stood chatting by the door to the shop. A few metres away, I stopped and tried to get my bearings.

'I have no idea who's performing tonight, but there's always something going on there.'

The lieutenant noticed me. I hid my face by politely touching my hat brim and moved on. How different everything looked with the daylight gone! The dark button shop, the fence with the black V, painted over white by the Wehrmacht. Mine were the only footsteps. I hurried across the square. There were still lights in some windows, but the blackout was about to start. I found the sign for the horse butcher's and laughed with relief. One more right—and at last I was standing in front of the damaged building. I hurried inside, felt under the stairs in the dark, grabbed the handle of my bag. With nervous hands, I changed my clothes. My wet socks didn't want to fit inside my boots. I jumped and stamped, buttoning my uniform coat at the same time.

My hobnailed heels resounded on the pavement; without haste, the corporal made his way back to his hotel. I crossed paths with the Luftwaffe group again and saluted.

Back in my room, I fell on the bed and folded my arms behind my head. Everything inside me was racing so fast, I couldn't think. A few centimetres away, scarcely muffled by the thin wall, someone was talking on the telephone. 'Well, if you bring the sisters, I won't call Dorine.' A brief laugh. 'You've really taken on quite a lot! Let's say nine-thirty, then?' The phone was hung up, and then I heard the dial rotating. I stared at the illuminated rectangle in the building across the street. My watch showed exactly eight o'clock. *'Est-ce que je pourrais parler avec Mademoiselle Dorine? Elle n'est pas là? Quoi?'* The window grew dark.

5

'Who taught you how to remove a carburetor?'
'Qui t'a appris comment on démonte un carburateur?'
'Je sais le faire,' the boy replied.
'I just know how to.'
'Who showed you how?'
'Qui t'a montré?'
'Je ne sais plus.'

'I can't remember.'

'Friends?'

'Maybe.'

'School friends, or grown-ups?'

'I can't remember.'

The captain sat on the edge of the desk and swung his boot back and forth. 'You should make an effort,' he said softly.

They had practically drowned the boy in the tub. They'd also dislocated three more of his fingers. The doctor was a second lieutenant, a thickset man with a goatee and manicured hands. He didn't give the boy any sort of anesthetic before pressing his finger joints back into place. Without a cry, without a whimper, and without warning, the boy threw up. The doctor complained about the puke on his waistcoat. Afterward, the captain provided the delinquent with some details of the new tortures that awaited him. Only then did the boy confess to having stolen the carburetors. This information had no actual relevance. The registry office had long since requisitioned other buses for prisoner transport. What they really wanted to know was where the Resistance fighters were hiding. The two corporals took up their positions in front of the boy again. I turned my head away.

'Smoke break?' The captain was staring at me. Had he noticed that I'd closed my eyes? He gave me permission to leave the room. At first, I thought it was so I wouldn't be a witness. But then I saw from the look on his face that he was sparing my feelings. As we went out, I heard the first scream.

The captain was an Austrian named Leibold. In the interrogation room and behind the desk, he

29

appeared icy and harsh, but outside the office, he liked to talk about home. His fine-featured face looked lost under his bald crown. Almost daily, we stood for a while together at the end of the hall, where the windows gave onto an unlikely garden instead of the street. Roses were budding there, and wild vines crept up the walls like green down.

'I miss the mountains,' Leibold said, offering me a cigarette. 'Do you know the area around Sankt Wolfgang, in the Salzkammergut?' He talked about the animals he liked, about the flowers and fruit he'd picked. About upland meadows and lake villages, about the solitude and the sheer rock faces where you needed ropes and crampons. I blew smoke against the windowpane. While he spoke, I watched a one-armed man mow the grass with a scythe attached to the leather harness he wore.

Leibold fell silent, waiting for a reply. 'I'm a city person,' I confessed.

'Then you must like Paris.'

I flicked ash off my cigarette. 'Sometimes our presence here seems unreal.'

I noticed his watchful look and quickly corrected myself. 'Unreal, but justified.' My eyes roamed around the garden. 'How long do you suppose it took him to learn to use that scythe with one arm?'

Leibold stepped behind me. 'War is the mother of invention,' he said. Expensive cologne, a hint of moth powder. 'How do you spend your evenings, Roth?'

'In my hotel, mostly.' I didn't move.

'You never have any fun?'

I heard the crackling as he dragged on his cigarette.

'I read a lot.'

'That's not what I mean.'

'These . . . places, these bars, are too loud for me.'

'There are others.'

'I can't afford those.' I looked at him so unexpectedly that he turned his eyes aside.

'I'll show you such a bar sometime.' It sounded like an order. He straightened his back. 'The doctor should have had enough time to bring the kid around by now.'

'What will happen to him—afterward?' I ground out the cigarette butt under my shoe.

'Drancy,' Leibold answered. 'But that's not my decision.'

The prison camp in Drancy was filled to overflowing; firing squads freed up space for new arrivals. And trains left every day for the armament factories on the Rhine.

*   *   *

I spent the whole evening sitting in my room and reading. Later, I stared at the darkened windows. The man on the telephone next door declared that Dorine had failed to meet his expectations. Hirschbiegel, wallowing in his bath over my head, played 'Ma Pomme' on his gramophone eight times in a row.

The next afternoon, desire and curiosity overcame fear once again. I pulled the checkered suit out of the wardrobe, took a fresh shirt, and picked out a tie. When the sentry saw me with my laundry bag for the second time in two days, he made a joke about cleanliness, hoping to get a

31

laugh out of the toilet attendant. She said, *'Une bonne soirée,* 'err Corporal.'

I stepped out onto the street, walked to the passageway, and did my quick-change routine as smoothly as an actor. I laid out my street shoes, unlaced and ready, so I wouldn't have to take so much as a step in the dirty corridor in my stocking feet. Finally, I packed the parts of my uniform in the cloth bag in such a way that later I'd be able to take them out and put them on in the correct order.

I was Antoine again! Stepping lightly as I strolled down the street, I bought a flower just so I could hold it in my hand. Without ever getting too far from the river, I walked southeast, passed the two islands, and crossed over to the left bank of the river just before coming to the Gare d'Austerlitz.

Monsieur Antoine turned into rue Jacob and sat down in the Café Lubinsky, across the square from the barbershop. I ordered *un crème.* As there was no milk, they served me powdered milk in a little marmalade bowl with my coffee. I pushed my hat back on my head and waited. At the table next to me, a woman was telling a story about a sixteen-year-old girl from the neighbourhood who, out of unrequited love, had denounced a schoolmate. The girl wrote an anonymous letter to the German commanding general, the woman said. The military police showed up at three in the morning. The young man was able to make good his escape at the last minute, she explained. He got away over the rooftops.

I raised my head: Chantal's silhouette had appeared behind the glass panes of the barbershop. I kept my eyes glued to the entrance. After a few minutes, she stepped outside, shook some clumps of hair into a garbage can, and held the door for a customer. A grey-haired cop approached from the other side. They stood together, he gesticulating with his nightstick, she pushing her ringlets behind her ear. The cop put his hand to the brim of his cap, took his leave, and strolled on. Chantal went into the shop and spoke to the barber. They laughed.

The following afternoon, I realized she didn't work at the barbershop every day; I waited for her in vain. The day after that, she chatted with the friendly Jew who had the haberdashery shop next door. He was the father of the youngsters who played in the street. Since the SS major's visit, the barbershop seemed to be popular with the Germans. One afternoon, I counted four men in field grey uniforms waiting for a haircut.

At 7:05, Chantal would pull down the rolling shutters. A minute later, she'd appear out of the side alley, closing her handbag. Until that moment, I'd have to guess what dress she had on under the long white coat she wore for work. Then I could see whether I'd guessed right. One day, it was the green one with the pale blue stripes. On the next, a particularly warm day, she had chosen a dress with red polka dots; the skirt swung out around her legs as she walked. As soon as she passed the Lubinsky, I'd pay—without haste—wait until she was almost out of sight, and follow her. She didn't take the most direct route to rue de Gaspard; instead, she'd make a detour past the lycée and linger at newsstands, studying the headlines. She usually bought vegetables and picked up a loaf of bread. I watched her while she dawdled, drawing out the last minutes before the curfew so she could stay outside as long as possible. Finally—it would already be dark—she'd stop in front of the black gate, take a last look at the busy street, and disappear. I rarely followed her past this point. On the occasions when I did go through the entrance, I could hear Chantal's footsteps echoing up ahead. When she passed the big stone, the light coming from the bookshop provided me with a last glimpse of the colour of her dress.

Once she vanished from sight, my day was over, too. I crossed the Pont Royal, went into the abandoned building, slipped into my uniform and boots, and returned to my hotel. I'd encounter fathers rushing to be with their families and mothers pushing their baby carriages home at top speed. Around this time of day, Parisians had an irritated look in their eyes; instead of enjoying the evening, they were fearful of being found on the streets of their own city. I walked into the hotel, entered my name in the sentry's register, left a message for Hirschbiegel informing him that I was too tired to go out, and threw myself on the bed without removing my boots. Throughout that time, I slept very badly. If the telephone man on the other side of the wall didn't keep me awake, then the warning shots fired by the patrols enforcing the curfew did the job. I often heard screaming, but only in my dreams. The red spots on Chantal's dress glimmered in the grey hours before dawn.

6

Her name was Anna Rieleck-Sostmann, and she was unusually tall. She worked for Leibold, ostensibly as a typist, but in reality she was responsible for the organization of his entire department. The lower ranks, not one of whom had graduated from anything resembling high school, were glad to be under the direction of Anna Rieleck-Sostmann. She was the queen bee of Leibold's staff.

When I stepped into the courtyard during the break one afternoon, she spoke to me. 'I saw you,' she said. She was eating a sandwich on dark bread. Everyone else had to make do with French bread, the insubstantial white stuff we called *Luftbrot*, 'air bread.' What army stores could have supplied her with black bread? And I smelled liverwurst, real German liverwurst.

'You saw me?' I leaned on the projecting section of the wall. 'Don't we see each other every day?'

Although the weather was warm, Rieleck-Sostmann was wearing a calf-length coat of white fur, either rabbit or cat. Her pinned-up hair bobbed up and down as she chewed. I watched her jaw muscles.

'You go around in civilian clothes after work.' Her grey-green eyes scrutinized me curiously.

I shifted my weight onto both legs so I wouldn't fall over. I started feeling sick on the spot. 'You must have me confused with someone else,' I replied.

'Stop it,' she said, cutting me off. 'Only senior

35

officers are allowed to go out in civilian clothes, and then only with special permission.'

I knew the rules. Such offences were harshly punished, most recently with marching orders for the Eastern Front. 'I didn't know that,' I said, searching Rieleck-Sostmann's face.

'You're not eating anything,' Rieleck-Sostmann said.

'I don't eat until after work.'

'Because of the interrogations?' Her features didn't change, but I had the feeling that she was smiling at me. 'There was one fellow before you who would always get an upset stomach. A second lieutenant from Wiesbaden. He took pills for it. After he ran out of them, he got sick. Now he's in Smolensk.'

'Fräulein Rieleck, what you saw—'

'*Frau,*' she said, correcting me. 'My husband fell in combat.' She bit her lip. 'Why do you pretend to be a Frenchman?'

'I wanted to see . . . whether my French is good enough to fool the French.'

'Why?' she asked, unimpressed. 'You're not in the secret service.'

'An ill-considered joke,' I babbled. 'I did it only once.'

'You're a dreamer, Corporal. You're out of step with the times.' Rieleck-Sostmann crumpled up her waxed sandwich paper and got to her feet. Her high heels made her taller than I was. 'Leibold's invited you to the Waffen-SS meeting, hasn't he?'

I felt hot and cold. 'Why do you say that?'

'Because I typed the guest list.'

Despite my fear, this announcement made me curious. 'Then do you also know why the captain would invite *me*?'

'Look in the mirror, Corporal.' For the first time, she smiled. 'Do you own a decent uniform for going out? Or do you want to show up at the gathering in your *checkered suit*?'

'Please, Frau Rieleck,' I said in a low voice. 'Don't turn me in.' She was silent. I said, 'I have a second uniform.'

'Be sure it's not missing a single button. By the way, the party's in your hotel.' She left me standing there.

In the interrogation room, in the corridor, in the office while I typed up reports, I searched my colleagues' faces. Had Rieleck-Sostmann informed on me? Did anyone else know about my masquerade? I went so far as to initiate a conversation with one of Leibold's bone breakers.

'Düsseldorf,' he said, surprised by my question about where he came from. Another SS corporal came up, and soon four of us were having a smoke together. During the chitchat about the Rhineland, I was relieved to note that at least the lower ranks didn't suspect a thing.

*   *   *

'My adjutant's home on leave,' Leibold said that same afternoon. He was looking out the window at the rain falling on the garden. Green foliage covered half the wall. 'I'd like you to accompany me,' he added with a smile.

I inquired as to the reason for the meeting.

'Camaraderie.' He let his cigarette butt fall right in front of my feet. 'Polish your insignia, Roth, and shine your boots.'

Back at the hotel, I got the better of my two uniforms out of the wardrobe and found it wrinkled. The laundry had closed some time ago, so I hurried down to the basement and asked the toilet attendant for advice. She was glad to help. Later that evening, the uniform, freshly pressed, was hanging next to the mirror. I put on the coat and inspected myself; the dark grey gave me a certain distinction. I snapped the forage cap onto my head and yanked my leather belt tight and straight.

In the lobby, dozens of officers, many of them escorting ladies, were mingling. Halting French, stilted atmosphere. Leibold came right on time.

'Not bad,' he said, looking me over. 'Black would look even better on you.' He slapped me on the shoulder. We didn't take the elevator—Leibold detested being closed up in narrow spaces.

We reached the fifth floor. General exchange of greetings. Two Gestapo agents bent over the guest list. They stared suspiciously at me, a Wehrmacht corporal in SS land. I stepped close to Leibold to make it clear I belonged there.

'I'll let you know when I need you,' he said. He left me by the entrance and joined the brass in the salon. I'd never seen a full colonel close up before. A giant of a man, he gave Leibold a hearty greeting. I ordered myself a glass of white wine and withdrew into a corner. Half an hour later, Anna Rieleck-Sostmann appeared. She was wearing a grey suit; its skirt covered her calves almost all the way to her ankles.

'You got an invitation, too?' I asked her, surprised.

'Telegram for Leibold,' Rieleck-Sostmann

replied, holding up a briefcase. Her look said that she wanted to distinguish herself from the painted and powdered French women the officers were gathered around.

'Shall I lead you to him?'

Leibold was sitting in the salon, across from the colonel. It was strange to see the two of them there, against a background of wallpaper decorated with a pattern of crowns. As I started toward them, I felt Rieleck-Sostmann's hand on my sleeve.

'There's time,' she said. Her fingers lingered on my cuff links. 'What floor is your room on?'

I told her.

'And the number?'

I looked at her.

'You go ahead. I'll knock twice,' she said. Her eyes remained cool.

'And if Leibold—'

'He won't miss you so soon.'

I wanted to say something in reply, but Rieleck-Sostmann's manner ruled out any protest. Slowly, I turned toward the double door, kept going, one step after another, without looking back. When I passed the watchdogs, I lifted my hand in salute. I could feel the sweat inside the shafts of my boots. My uniform coat was stuck to my armpits. On the stairs, a group of SS officers were trying to form a difficult French sentence. I hastened down three flights and through the hall. A lightbulb gave me a fright, popping and going out as I passed it. I opened my door, let it shut behind me, and stood in the room like a stranger. The bed took up practically the whole room. I neither turned on the light nor opened the curtains, even though the air was stale. As usual, there was nothing to drink. I felt a muffled drumming in my temples.

A short while later, Rieleck-Sostmann slipped into the room and closed the door without a sound. She looked at me like someone assessing a commodity and loosened her hair. With a single grab, she unfastened the buckle of my leather belt. 'A bayonet would look good on you,' she said as she laid the gear aside.

'I find daggers unpractical,' I murmured. 'It's too easy to get tangled up.'

She gave me a push, and I fell onto the bed. Then she unbuttoned her jacket and blouse, but she didn't take them off. With a high, clear sound, her skirt slid to the floor. She was wearing flesh-coloured hose. She knelt over me and undid my shirt. I thought of my neighbour in the next room, who perhaps at that very moment was picking up the receiver on the other side of the thin wall. I said, 'We have to be quiet.'

She grabbed me by the hips and pulled my trousers down to my knees. It made me think about the water washing over the steel framework of the Pont Solférino.

7

The two Gestapo agents conscientiously checked their list before they let me back into the meeting rooms.

Leibold was waiting. 'You must ask permission to leave,' he said irritably.

'Latrine visit, Captain,' I said, coming to

attention. When he looked away, I wiped the perspiration off my upper lip.

'You just have to hang on for another half hour. Then we're going to Turachevsky's with a few of these gentlemen.'

'I can't afford to go to a nightclub, Capt—'

'Stop with the whining,' Leibold snapped. 'You think they bill champagne by the glass? I'm not interested in going out with a tight-ass. Try some of the sturgeon.'

I spread a bit of the black jelly on a rusk. Since the Soviet embassy got cleared out, tinned food was everywhere. Also different kinds of tea, richer and stronger than the ground powder provided by the Wehrmacht. I remembered reading horror stories about the confiscations in *Je suis partout*. Trapdoors and dungeons, electrified tubs for burning bodies. The faces in the photographs, bleached white by the flash.

I walked around unobtrusively, plate in hand, among the crowd of uniforms. Looking out the window, I could see a Frenchwoman in a robe, standing on the balcony across the street and gazing at the noisy gathering. When I leaned out, she disappeared into the darkness of her apartment. I stared at the dark rectangle. What was Chantal doing at that moment? Did she live with her father? Was their flat above the bookstore? For the first time, I wondered why I'd never yet seen her with a man. The barber, perhaps?

'Are you dreaming, Roth?'

The champagne made Leibold's normally melancholy eyes glitter. 'We're off,' he said, putting on his cap. When his bald pate was covered up, he looked years younger.

Four SS officers were going to share the car. Mine was the only Wehrmacht uniform. Things threatened to be a bit tight in the backseat, so I offered to take the Métro, suggesting that we could meet up again at the Trinité stop. Leibold brushed off that idea with a joke: They wouldn't want to throw me in with all the common soldiers hurrying to get back to their quarters before lights-out, he said. When I got in the car, the colonel looked peeved. Leibold unbuckled his dagger and laid it on his knee. I pressed myself up against the door.

'Do you know what I found on my way out of the officers' mess?' the colonel asked. 'A brochure.'

We drove off.

The second lieutenant in the front seat turned around. 'Indecent photos?'

'Indecent but amusing,' the colonel said with a laugh. 'A woman, shot from behind, wearing nothing but a pair of short lederhosen. They had oval windows cut in them, and the cheeks of her butt were showing through!'

During the ensuing laughter, Leibold observed me with searching eyes. We passed the Pont Solférino. The invisible water roared.

'Now's the best time for Turachevsky's,' the lieutenant in the front seat said. 'After midnight, the Wehrmacht starts drifting in. Then the couches tend to get crowded. One night, I counted eight grunts sitting on a single sofa.' His bleating laugh was smothered by a look from the colonel.

'I heard a Negro sing there once,' Leibold said. 'Totally amazing.'

'I hope there's a dance show tonight,' the

colonel replied.

They fell silent until we got to rue de Clichy. The streets were practically empty. There were a few German civilians and a woman in a hurry. Her wooden sandals clattered as she ran. When she heard the German car, she disappeared into a building. A blue light burning in the entrance to the Scheherazade reflected off the visor of the night porter's cap.

We stopped in front of Turachevsky's. I jumped out and opened the captain's door.

'Don't make such a face,' Leibold hissed.

Before the second lieutenant could lay a hand on the doorbell, the door was opened.

'What's this? The place is empty.' The colonel looked all around. 'Usually, you have to ring like crazy before they can hear you.'

I was the last to enter the lobby. Sofas and chaise longues. High overhead, a chandelier glittered in the smokeless air.

'It's early yet,' the colonel muttered.

The woman who greeted guests came toward us, wearing a blue silk dress. In one hand, she clutched a wadded-up lace handkerchief, which she was drumming against her forehead. 'Ah, *mon Dieu,* good evening, what ees up, holy smoke?' she cried out. 'Where arc your friends, *les messieurs soldats?*'

The officers looked at one another.

'It's so lovely and warm out, madame, such a fine evening. People prefer to stay outside.'

'But what you talking, *m'sieur l'officier*? All soldier have gone to Russia, gone last night, on the railroad.'

'Damned nonsense!' the colonel cut in. *'Je vous*

43

assure, madame, no German soldier is leaving Paris for the east. Who starts these bloody latrine rumours?'

'Hopefully, you are right,' madame replied, somewhat relieved. *'Encore deux jours comme ça et je dois congédier les filles.'* She fanned her bosom with the handkerchief. *'Quelle horreur, cette guerre de Russie.* They say Germans have lost many men.'

'On the contrary, madame.' The colonel adopted a severe tone. *'Il faut garder votre sangfroid, je vous en prie.* The German losses are meagre when compared with the world-historical dimensions of our successes.' With that, he left the matron's side, stalked resonantly across the room, and disappeared into the bar. Our convoy fell in behind him.

Civilians from the embassies, one of them wearing gaiters. The other civilians were rip-off artists, black marketeers, and pimps. Very few Wehrmacht, but many SS, with their black uniforms and death's-head insignia. Terse nods, careless salutes. The waiter showed us to the best table—the stage was only an arm's length away. I hesitated before taking a seat. Leibold gave me a comradely wave.

'Down in front,' someone behind me shouted.

I pulled up a chair from a neighbouring table. On the stage, dancing girls were performing an animal scene. They wore sheep masks and lion masks and very little else. The band played folk melodies. While the girls hopped about, the colonel ordered two bottles. 'If the champagne's as stale as this is . . .' he grumbled.

At the end of the number, the lions lay down with the lambs. The Wehrmacht contingent howled approval.

'Easy to please,' the big officer said, looking around condescendingly.

Without bowing, the girls disappeared from the stage. The band played a march. The pianist stood up and announced in broken German that 'living nude sculptures' were next on the evening's programme.

'I'm going to need schnapps for that!' the colonel groaned. Not waiting for the waiter to open the champagne bottles, he sent him off to fetch something stronger. The second lieutenant popped the corks. Leibold's hand hung at his side, not far from my knee. He was beating time on the leg of my chair. I took a full glass and shifted a little to one side.

' "Nude sculptures!" ' bleated the lieutenant as four girls presented *The Bridge to Happiness* on the stage. A young man in princely garments crossed the bridge, attentively considering each of its four naked piers. The colonel poured himself some schnapps.

'This is worse than *Grimm's Fairy Tales*!'

'Well, yes, but the one with the chignon sure is a hot-looking little beast.' The second lieutenant was alternating between schnapps and champagne. *The Bridge to Happiness* disappeared. Accompanied by a fiddle solo, the models for the next living sculpture took up their positions. I felt Leibold's hand gripping my bootleg.

Three young women presented *The Judgment of Paris*. Naked Greek goddesses, bearing their symbols and turning slowly in a circle. The bosomy Hera wore a red toga. Aphrodite played with a fig leaf, clumsily covering each of her naked parts in

45

turn. The third was Pallas Athena.

I forgot Leibold's hand, which was carefully encircling my knee, because the girl playing the war goddess was Chantal. She wore a helmet and armor, the latter cut so as to show her breasts to great advantage. Like the others, she stretched out her arm to the golden apple and turned in a circle. Her reddish brown hair gleamed in the spotlight. Her face was completely expressionless.

'That's enough for me, gentlemen!' The colonel sprang to his feet. 'I'm going to have them *appeler les dames.*' He stamped back into the salon.

Very slowly, very stiffly, I stood up, staring fixedly at the stage. Leibold's hand withdrew and moved toward his cigarette case. Paris, in gold makeup, was about to hand the apple to Aphrodite, but the commotion in front of the stage irritated him. He dropped the apple, which rolled behind the footlights. Merriment among the goddesses. Without finishing the scene, they disappeared behind the transparent curtain. The band played 'Liebeslied.' The stage lights went out. I kept staring. Chantal, the barber's assistant—had she really been standing there?

Leibold scrutinized me. 'Which of the Graces has struck your fancy? Or was it perhaps the young man?' I registered his soft face, the drops of sweat on his forehead.

'So what's going on?' asked the second lieutenant.

Leibold pointed toward the salon, where a bell was being rung for the second time. Without saying anything, I made my way among the tables. Leibold followed, glass in hand.

When we entered the room, madame was

46

clapping for the girls to hurry up. They were already entering through every door. The chandelier shone more brightly. The colonel was on the sofa, waiting to review the selection. A tall girl in a blue tunic placed herself in the centre, like a flagpole that the others gathered around. A second girl, looking insulted, lifted her little skirt and gave us a rear view. There was a Slavic girl with yellowish eyes and powerful teeth and a girl in a green shirt, very thin, with pronounced shoulder blades. More girls kept coming in, their faces long from suppressed yawns. The rustle of silk. The squeaking of high-heeled sandals. My eyes flew from door to door. Which door would Chantal come through?

'What do you suppose this snaggletoothed battle-axe is up to?' The colonel laughed. 'She's even mobilized the reserves!' One girl on the flank opened her kimono. Her breasts stared dully in opposite directions. It struck me that not one of these women seemed to be really present. Their smiles looked painted on with spit and lipstick. There were two rows of them now, one behind the other.

'I always thought they had at most ten women here,' the big officer said, nodding, impressed.

The second lieutenant was exchanging glances with the tall girl in the tunic. After the second row was full, the latecomers lay down in front of the others. Raised eyebrows, serious expressions. Chantal's eyes were not among them.

'Attention, group photograph!' the colonel cried out, baring his teeth. He undid his top button and pulled at his Merit Cross. The second lieutenant was waiting for his commanding officer to make

47

his choice so that he, the lieutenant, could finally snap up the tall girl and vanish. Leibold lounged in an armchair, as though nothing that was happening had anything to do with him. Silence fell; the moment of decision had arrived.

'*Mesdames, l'offre surpasse le . . .*' The colonel turned to me. 'How do you say *demand*?'

'*Demande,*' I answered, thereby drawing all eyes.

Madame brought champagne. Leaning over the colonel, she called his attention to a full-figured angel. '*Vous connaissez cette fille,* Flora, a recent addition?'

'No, no, not her.' Flora failed to suit the officer's taste. He said, 'The one behind her, in the second row. Fourth from the left, with the vulgar mouth. We've already had the pleasure.'

'*Alors, monsieur,*' madame said with a nod. She waved her handkerchief in the direction of the chosen one.

'Yes, I have simple German tastes. I like plain food,' the colonel mused as the girl moved toward him, her eyes cast down. 'All right,' he said with a sigh, as though he'd lost interest in the remainder of the process. The second lieutenant jumped on the tunic a bit too eagerly, as though someone else might snatch her away from him. She didn't smile.

'Lost your appetite?' Leibold stood next to me. I whiffed his expensive cologne.

'I really didn't plan on—'

'We could go somewhere else, if you want.' He took hold of the brocade trim on my collar. His arm brushed the back of my neck. I looked into his white, tactless face. Two dozen women were still facing us. Madame played with the silver cross on her bosom. Her expression was supposed to be

48

encouraging, but I could see her impatience. In the second row, a girl with bobbed hair yielded to a yawn; her mouth opened wide. She rubbed her eyes with her hand, making her bracelets tinkle.

'Her,' I said, and stepped away from Leibold.

Softly murmuring *'Pardon'* and leading with her narrow shoulders, the girl with the bobbed hair parted the ranks of her colleagues. Leibold didn't stop smiling for a second as he made his way back to the bar.

The girls turned on their heels. Those who were on the floor stood up. There was a whirling of sleeves and belt ends. And then the room and the grey-green carpet were empty. On the stairs, the unchosen began to talk all at once, like girls in a boarding school. The one with the bobbed hair waited for me to accompany her. She put her hand in front of her mouth. All this while, I was trying to identify Chantal among the girls leaving the room, but my hopes were in vain. The bookshop owner's daughter. The Judgment of Paris.

'Veuillez monter?' madame suggested encouragingly.

I followed the bobbed head without touching its owner, who introduced herself, as I might have expected, as 'Yvette.' I knew that Leibold was watching me from inside the door to the bar, so I didn't turn around again.

The room was bigger than I'd imagined. I sank down onto the bed. Yvette took off her little green coat.

'Seulement un moment,' I said.

She didn't understand and knelt down on the carpet in front of me.

'Je pars tout de suite,' I said. I fished some

49

banknotes out of my breast pocket, paid her, and pushed her hands away.

'*Mais qu'est-ce que t'as? Tu me voulais.*'

'*Oui, tu me plais beaucoup. Je suis fatigué.*'

I looked at my watch. Was Chantal still in the building? How did she get from Pigalle to rue de Gaspard at night? Somewhere behind a nearby wall, the second lieutenant laughed. The girl with the bobbed hair laid her head in my lap. She was still stroking my hand when she fell asleep.

8

'Tonight! This evening! Please!' Hirschbiegel bellowed, banging on my door. Then, all of a sudden, he was standing in the doorway.

'Tonight we're doing the town!' he cried out. He stared wide-eyed, trying to make me out in the darkness.

Hirschbiegel weighed two hundred and twenty-five pounds. His legs were as thick as barrels, and he was as strong as an ox. Although he had his lieutenant's uniforms custom-made, he still looked like a caricature in them.

'*Cherchez la femme!*' he shouted. 'You're not going to stand me up this time!'

Hirschbiegel came from Munich. His parents were rich. He said they even owned an apartment in Paris. As far as their son was concerned, the war was a cakewalk. The only thing that caused him anxiety was the thought of going into whorehouses alone. He was ashamed to speak to the grisettes and wanted me to smooth his path for him.

'Not tonight,' I said, pulling the covers up over my chest.

'Good God! All you do is lie around!' In one step, he reached the window and yanked the curtains aside. Droplets of sweat gleamed in his curly blond hair. He turned around and froze.

Anna Rieleck-Sostmann braced one leg against the edge of the bed and rolled up her stocking.

'Holy Christ!' Hirschbiegel exclaimed, so shocked, he toppled against the wall. 'I beg your pardon! It was so dark in here.' Even as he excused himself, he was blatantly ogling the half-naked woman. 'I didn't know you were in contact with the enemy,' he said, grinning. 'Introduce me.' He'd already recovered all his former bearishness. 'Maybe the three of us could—'

'Leave the room while a lady gets dressed,' Rieleck-Sostmann said. Her tone had the same effect on Hirschbiegel as it unfailingly had on the SS corporals in the office. The sounds of his native tongue further disconcerted him. 'She's one of ours!' he blurted out.

'Get out now, Lieutenant,' Rieleck-Sostmann said. She didn't raise her voice at all.

'If I had only known ... Please accept my apologies, Fräulein.' He groped for the door behind his back with one large pawlike hand. As he retreated, he banged into the bed, and Rieleck-Sostmann sat up menacingly. Immediately thereafter, we could hear the lieutenant's heavy steps echoing down the hall.

'Sorry about that,' I said, touching her back.

'Nothing to be done. Your hotel is still less complicated than mine.' She smoothed the second stocking and looked at me. Her blond hair covered

51

half her face. 'Are you going to go out with him?'

I took one of her cigarettes. 'Maybe.'

She began pinning up her hair. 'Don't you ever get the itch to play the Frenchman again?' she asked.

I struck a match. 'Suppose I did. What harm would it do?'

'Well, I might denounce you as a *déserteur amoureux.*'

I could never tell when she was joking. She looked into my eyes as they reflected the match's bright flame. On a sudden impulse, she got to her feet, opened the wardrobe, and took out the suit with the little checks. She smiled as she put on the jacket. Disguised as a man, she came back to the bed and sank down on me. I endured her painful attentions. Afterward, she stood up and let the jacket slip to the floor. Aided by the mirror, she arranged her hair for the second time. I ran my tongue over my lower lip, feeling the spot where she had bitten me.

In the seconds it took Rieleck-Sostmann to make sure the hotel corridor was clear, I wished for nothing so much as normal duty far from Paris, for some office somewhere, for written sentences I could translate into German. And at the same time, I knew I'd never have it so easy anywhere else.

Rieleck-Sostmann left. For several minutes, I stared at the jacket on the carpet. I missed Monsieur Antoine. The young man who pushed his hat high on his forehead and walked through the city in soft-soled shoes. The unknown Parisian who greeted people and was greeted in turn. He enjoyed soaking up some of the warmth of this summer afternoon.

Until that day, I hadn't had the courage to disregard Rieleck-Sostmann's warning. I hadn't gone back to rue Jacob, not in civilian clothes, not in my uniform. Sometimes I considered dropping into Turachevsky's, but I couldn't bring myself to do that, either. I often brooded over Chantal's presence there and tried to make sense of it. I didn't know much about her, but one thing was obvious: She hated the occupiers. Why would she appear before them naked?

I had grown gloomy and apathetic in these past weeks. We interrogated a Gascon suspected of plotting the arson attack in the ninth arrondissement. He was taciturn, gnarled as a root, and good at hiding behind his country dialect. I often had to repeat questions before I could understand what he meant. Leibold turned this man over to the SS corporals, but it was as though they were pounding on insensible stone. The Gascon had massive shoulders that he hunched defensively when the blows began. He let the corporals thrust his head into the tub. They held him under the water interminably, but when they pulled him back up, he said nothing. They prevented him from sleeping; heavy-lidded, his jaw jutting forward, he sat there and spoke so unintelligibly that I was obliged to work out for myself much of what he said.

'We'll never get anything useful out of this guy,' Leibold said later, when we were in the hall. 'But I'm sure he's got important connections. I'll let him go in a few days. Then I'll set five bloodhounds on his trail. From then on, he'll never be alone, not for a second. At some point, he's got

53

to try to make contact again.'

Sometimes I persuaded myself that I could be present at the endless interrogations—and even that I could witness the corporals' *techniques*—without feeling anything. And then again, I thought I couldn't bear it. The memory of the screams woke me up every night. I'd tried to talk to Leibold about getting transferred back to my old unit; I'd pointed out that my assignment to the SS was only temporary. I shouldn't get any ideas in my head was his reply.

'Have you been back to Turachevsky's recently?' Leibold asked. We'd avoided this subject ever since that night. 'And what about your little thing with the bobbed hair? Was she an open-minded girl?' He had a cold, lascivious gleam in his eye.

My days in rue de Saussaies, my sexual gymnastics with Rieleck-Sostmann, my yearning for Chantal—I felt I was caught in a joyless triangle.

There was a sound of rushing water over my head now. Hirschbiegel was getting into his bathtub. I kept staring at the jacket on the floor. The thought that the strains of 'Ma Pomme' would become audible at any moment gave me the necessary impetus. I quickly picked up my pants from the bed and started to dress.

The air was still hot, even though evening was coming on. I transformed myself into Monsieur Antoine, taking along my volume of La Fontaine, just as I'd done the first time. The book made me feel more secure. I wasted no time on the Right Bank, crossed the Pont Royal, and headed for rue Jacob. At the Café Lubinsky, a table in the shade was free, and I ordered my first *café crème*. I laid the book open in front of me like a man who wanted to read undisturbed. From one day to the next, the weather had turned quite warm. The air above the hot pavement was shimmering. Haze hung around the gables. The people were enjoying the heat. I heard them talking about the thunderstorms that would descend on the city during the night. I bent over to tie the laces on one of my shoes. And then I felt a shadow.

She stood over me in grave contemplation, wearing the dress with the red dots. She wasn't staring at me; she was examining my book. A fierce monkey rode on the back of a dragon-fish in the midst of a foaming dark-green sea. For me, that copperplate engraving on the title page had always been the entrance to an enchanted place. Chantal's fingers touched the hairs of the fish-monster's beard.

'Only a catfish looks like this,' she said. 'No other animal.' Her voice was surprisingly deep, like a boy's when it's breaking.

'I've never seen a catfish,' I said. It was the first time I'd ever used the expression *poisson-chat.*

'My grandfather catches them sometimes,' Chantal replied. 'In the country.'

'You live in the country?'

She gave me a surprised look. 'You know I don't.' She sat down so abruptly that my coffee sloshed out of its cup. She recited, ' *'Une grenouille vit un boeuf / Qui lui sembla de belle taille.'* ' Then she opened the book.

'The frog and the ox,' I said, nodding. 'Do you like that fable?' I was searching for the story between the lines.

'It comes up a lot.'

'The frog who wants to be as big as an ox?'

'People who puff themselves up until they burst.' She called out her order to the passing waiter. 'I haven't seen you here for a long time,' she said. She squeezed her dress between her knees. My eyes strayed over the triangle formed by her lap.

'You noticed me before?'

There was a pause. Then she said, 'Most visitors to Paris wear a uniform. Not you.'

'Not me.' I waited. A puff of wind stirred the pages. The book was now open to 'The Monkey and the Leopard.' The waiter put a glass of lemonade in front of Chantal. She drank in tiny sips. My eyes penetrated inside her mouth.

'What kind of work do you do?' she suddenly asked.

I bought a little time by closing the *Fables* and putting the volume back into my pocket. Pretending to be a bookseller would be too risky. A bookseller's daughter would know what questions to ask. The Sorbonne was closed—I knew that—but what about the universities outside of Paris? The pause threatened to go on too long.

'I'm a student.'

'That's exactly what you look like.' For the first time, she smiled. 'Why didn't you have to join the army?'

'And what about you, mademoiselle?' I said. I'd had enough of Twenty Questions. 'Do you do anything besides sweep up hair?'

'What do you mean by that?' There was a bit of tiny fuzz on her upper lip.

'I know something about you.' I snapped my fingers and pointed to my empty cup. The waiter nodded. I looked at Chantal. 'You like butterflies.'

56

'How do you . . .' she started to ask, genuinely surprised.

'Every time a butterfly flies away, you feel a little sad.'

Silence reigned. I could feel my heart beating. At that moment, I felt capable of anything, even of walking across the power line that passed over the café.

'How do you know that?' Her eyes were serious.

'Do you dance?' I heard the soft laughter in my voice. 'Surely you know a place where there's dancing tonight.'

'There's a blackout.'

'Where there's dancing *behind drawn curtains.*'

'What about the curfew?'

'The Krauts can't be everywhere.' I said it in French: *les boches.*

Her glass was empty. She looked inside her purse. 'You're wrong about me. I have to go.'

'May I?' I reached for the saucer with the chits.

'Do you know the fable of the amorous fox?' Chantal asked, standing up. 'The fox is in love with a girl. She promises to love him in return, under one condition. He has to cut his claws and have his teeth filed down. The amorous fox does as she orders. And now, since he can't defend himself any longer, the girl sets her dogs on him.'

I put some coins on the saucer.

'Do you mean a fox shouldn't let a girl tame him?'

Without answering, she turned and left, squeezing past the other tables. I put on my hat and followed her. The waiter in the Lubinsky stared in wonder at the departing guest who'd paid for his coffee but hadn't drunk it. Chantal went

57

west on rue Jacob.

'Do you have to go home already?' I asked as I caught up with her.

The first thunder rumbled in the east.

'What else do you know about me?' She walked faster.

'In the evening, you go to the news shop and read the news. You even read the front page of *Je suis partout.* You buy fruit at Mallard's and bread at the bakery two doors farther on. You push the black gate open and step into the hidden street and disappear. Sometimes you sit on a big rock that looks as though it must have fallen from heaven.'

Chantal stopped walking. In the distance, a blue-white bolt of lightning ripped the milky sky.

'My father says a man was asking after me. Was that you?'

The next clap of thunder burst over the fifth arrondissement. Suddenly, the sky was dark. The air was filled with the smell of sulphur. A swift shadow split Chantal's face into two halves. A gust of wind threatened to carry my hat away. She came very close to me. 'If my father sees your La Fontaine, I'm sure he'll offer to buy it.'

'It's not for sale.'

Lightning flashed over the rooftops. The dusty wind pressed Chantal's dress against her hips. I took off my checkered coat and hung it over her shoulders. The first raindrops spattered on my shirt.

'We shouldn't stay here.'

We ran toward the storm, which was howling down the narrow street. Chantal's hair was dishevelled and blown about. 'Shall I walk you home?'

The wind blew dust in my face, making me spat. Chantal turned her head away. I put my arm around her back, and together we braced ourselves against the wind. At the intersection with the boulevard, we suddenly collided with a wall of rain. Chantal immediately pulled me into a bumpy side street. Its surface was split, as though damaged by an earthquake. After about a dozen steps, we came to a little wine bar. It was packed with people standing quite close together, taking refuge from the storm.

The bartender spotted us. 'Red or white?' he asked.

I looked into Chantal's flushed face. She shook out her hair. I closed my eyes at the spray of rainwater. 'Two reds!' she called back.

The glasses were handed over the bar and from one customer to the next before coming into Chantal's hands. 'Where do you live?' she asked.

I hadn't anticipated this question. I couldn't possibly tell her the name of my hotel. I thought about Hirschbiegel. 'I stay in a friend's apartment,' I said. He had described the flat to me once. It was in the second arrondissement. A very comfortable place, according to him; you could invite women up there.

We clinked glasses. She sipped her wine. 'Where is this apartment?'

'In the second.'

Chantal drank her wine in silence. A fine steam rose from her hair. The moth powder in my jacket exuded a peculiar smell. More escapees from the rain crowded in. You could hardly see out the tavern window. Chantal grew tired. Her shoulders sagged against mine. I put my arm around her waist, turned her toward me a little, and took the back of her head in my hands. Her eyes were closed. I touched her lips; they opened easily. I felt the stream of her breath and her fingertips in my back. The man beside us jostled us and suggested we lean on someone else. Chantal's eyelids opened. Violet and grey in her pupils. She felt with one hand for the nape of my neck. Nearby, someone shook out his wet coat. A woman laughed. The smell of wine, of humanity.

'What do you do when you're not reading the *Fables*?' Chantal asked.

I had a vision of the interrogation room, the bound prisoners. The ones who tried to haggle with Leibold in order to spare themselves pain. The weak ones, who revealed all they knew and were mistreated out of sheer contempt. The steadfast ones, who bonded with their pain and broke down all the same.

'I just live in Paris,' I said. Shortly after that, we left. The sky was clearing as we stepped outside. The heat of the day radiated from the walls. Chantal and I walked side by side, without touching. We reached the black gate.

'What are you doing tomorrow?' I asked.

She gave me back my jacket. 'I'm not in the salon tomorrow,' she said.

For a moment, I thought about Turachevsky's, about her performance as Pallas Athena. Then I realized she meant the *salon de coiffure*, the barbershop.

'Shall we meet at Café Lubinsky?'

'I don't know.' Her eyes searched mine.

'Or would you rather meet in a park?'

'Aren't you cold?' she asked.

I held the heavy door open for her, and she stepped through. Before she reached the streetlight, everything went dark. But I was happy as I hastened through the ghostly, unlighted streets. Monsieur Antoine had spent an evening with Chantal. No disguise, no playacting—it had been me, me myself!

9

The next evening, I climbed the stairs to the floor above and opened the door while I was still knocking on it. I'd just heard the boots fly into the corner, and the gramophone had played 'Ma Pomme' once already. Hirschbiegel had come home.

'Hirschbiegel, it's me.' The sound of running water; he was in the bathtub. I circled the bed and knocked on the bathroom door.

'Hirschbiegel?'

I pushed the door slightly open. There he was. His huge body threatened to burst the tub. His wet, hairy chest swelled up out of the water. His eyes were closed.

'Hey, Lieutenant!'

His response was a bloodcurdling scream and terrified eyes.

'Why did you creep up on me like that?' Drops of water glistened in his curly blond hair. He braced his arms on the side of the tub and started to pull himself up, accompanied by much cracking and creaking.

'No enemy in sight, Hirschbiegel,' I said, sitting down on the tiny stool.

'Did the lady you were with yesterday eventually calm down?' He tilted his head, pressing his fat chin to one side. 'What unit is she attached to?'

'She's only a casual acquaintance,' I said. I wanted to keep Rieleck-Sostmann out of this.

'And how are things with the ladies otherwise?'

'Pickings are rather slim at the moment.'

'Your blonde Valkyrie is anything but slim,' he said, full of admiration.

'Comrade-love,' I said.

Hirschbiegel laughed out loud. 'Comradeship is a wonderful thing!' His body rolled over in the tub. 'When are you going to take me along on one of your forays?'

'I really don't like going to the bordellos anymore,' I said, shrugging my shoulders. 'They rob you of your illusions.'

The red face nodded gravely. 'You're hungry for company, but you can only be a stranger, a foreigner.' Suddenly, he braced himself on the sides of the bathtub. 'I made you the offer!' he cried out. 'Haven't I told you more than once that the flat is at your disposal?'

I observed the pattern in the tiles. 'Right, you have mentioned that.'

'If you'd only help me a little,' he begged.

'How is it that your parents bought a place in Paris *before* the war?'

'My father's boyhood dream,' Hirschbiegel replied. 'Dad always wanted to be a painter. He ignored the fairy tales about our 'hereditary enemy' and bought the apartment back in the days of the Weimar Republic. The whole transaction was handled through a Jewish proxy—to this day, everything's under the name Wasserlof. A *Hirschbiegel* in Châtelet would be too conspicuous.' The lieutenant turned off the water tap with his toes. Sudden silence.

'So the apartment's empty?' I asked mildly.

'Isn't that a crying shame?' He sat up. 'The place isn't big, but there's enough room to have a good time. When can I show it to you?'

'Maybe tomorrow?' I said a touch too quickly.

The colossus rose from his bath with a mighty rush of water. 'What's up?' he asked, standing amid glittering fountains. 'First I hear nothing from you for weeks, and now you're in a hurry?' He reached for the towel.

'The war can't go on forever.' I looked out the window.

With one foot still in the tub, he looked at me. 'You're right. Pluck the rose before it fades. But I can't tomorrow. There's a situation review, and then in the evening there's bridge with the colonel.' Leaving a trail of damp streaks, he left the bathroom.

'Maybe I could'—I stood up slowly—'take a look at it all the same.'

'Without me?' His eyes narrowed suspiciously.

'Just to see what we'd need—to make it cosy.' I followed him.

He stepped over to the chest of drawers and took out a small, delicate-looking key, silver-plated and chased. 'You can enter the building at any time, but the concierge doesn't know you. You think she's going to let an enemy get past her?'

I considered telling him about Monsieur Antonie. 'That looks like a key for a display case,'

63

I said instead. 'Not for a flat.'

After a little hesitation, he pressed the key into my hand. 'Do you already have somebody in mind we could bring there for . . .' His face glowed hopefully.

'Shouldn't be a problem.' I went to the door.

'Wait a minute.' He came after me in his towel. 'You don't know where it is.'

I made a note of the address.

'And one more thing, Hirschbiegel,' I said, pointing to his gramophone. 'Please, please, put on another record.'

10

The following evening, for the first time and not without some second thoughts, I left my ID tags in the hotel room. More carefully than usual, I transformed myself into Monsieur Antoine. Near the bridge, I bought a rose and stuck it into my lapel as I crossed over. I returned the smiles of two ladies who were walking arm in arm. I didn't take the customary route; instead, I approached rue Jacob obliquely, in a series of loops. The hotel signs seemed like a promise. I was in possession of something better: the key to Hirschbiegel's apartment. I carried it in the lining of my suit coat.

I reached the Lubinsky by way of a side street and stepped onto the terrace, acting as though the reflecting facade of the barbershop across the way held no fascination for me whatsoever. My heart was pounding as I sat down. Although I knew

Chantal didn't work in the shop on Wednesdays, I tried to make her out through the storefront window. In my imagination, she was about to notice me, too, and come walking out the door. Any minute now.

The terrace was crowded. People were talking about the cease-fire; the Wehrmacht was observing it, they said, but not the SS. The night before, one of the fancy windows in the Hôtel Louis XV had been shot to pieces. I didn't drink coffee; I ordered pastis instead, thinning the oily liquid with water. The taste reminded me of childhood visits to the dentist. I drank pastis for Chantal. I had to become more French in everything; I wanted to please her, to make her laugh, to give her proof of my generosity. My thoughts wandered over her body. My hand remembered her waist, the resilience of her muscles. I had smelled her hair; what did her mouth taste like? Her back was straight, her legs strong. Throughout these reflections, my eyes kept searching up and down the street. Whenever I saw a green dress approaching, I squinted; the woman was never Chantal. After ordering a second glass, I went inside the café and looked in every room, every corner. At the end of an hour, I paid and left. I crossed the street on unsteady legs. Inside the shop, the barber was cutting a girl's hair. The only other person in the dimly lighted room was the old man with the newspaper.

Two women came toward me. One said, 'They don't send twelve-year-olds to prison camp.' The other wouldn't be consoled. 'Michel's fourteen,' she said.

They saw my reflection in a shop window. I

turned aside and sniffed my rose. At that moment, I spotted Chantal on the other side of the street, in the Lubinsky. She really had come; she'd taken our date seriously! I waved to her and started to walk back across the street. A military vehicle rattled past, hiding her from my sight for a few seconds. As though she hadn't noticed me, Chantal slipped between tables and left the café again. I called her name; she didn't turn around. I thought I'd catch up with her in a few strides, but she was faster. Whenever I tried to get closer to her, she picked up the pace; if I fell back, she went slower, too. I started running, determined to put an end to this incomprehensible game. Chantal turned into a narrow side street. It was a while before I caught sight of her again. After a series of such inexplicable manoeuvres, we were getting closer to rue de Gaspard, without having exchanged a single word. She pushed open the door in the gate and went in. Before it closed again, I stepped through as well, ran past the junk dealer's place, and saw Chantal disappear into the bookshop. Why had she led me here?

I reached the big rock and looked up at the entrance. Inside, Joffo was waiting on two sergeants who were buying picture postcards. I waited with mounting curiosity until the soldiers left the shop, and then I went in.

The bookseller was standing at the counter in the rear of the shop, arranging books into two stacks. No trace of Chantal. I set off the shop bell and wished him good evening. As I moved toward him, Joffo stepped to one side. For a moment, I lost sight of him. When I got to the counter, I cast a glance into the stockroom behind it, where I

66

figured Chantal was.

Someone grabbed me and forced my arms behind my back. Strong hands held me tightly. The attack came so unexpectedly, I banged my head on the counter. Gasping, I tried to turn around, but the iron grip I was in didn't yield at all. Two men pulled me upright and shoved me ahead of them. As I staggered, I recognized one of them as old Joffo. He and the other man took me into the stockroom. I braced my feet against the floorboards, tried to free my arms. A trapdoor in the floor stood open. They drove me toward the opening; I started to cry out, got pushed, staggered; they held on to me when I was on the verge of falling through. I struck my head against a beam and felt my feet stumbling down some stairs until I reached solid ground. Packed earth: a cellar. They set me on a chair. Now I recognized the second man—it was the barber from rue Jacob. He skillfully tied my hands behind my back while Joffo closed the trapdoor above us. Cutting pain in my wrists. I straightened up a little and stared into the light of a single swaying lightbulb.

'Welcome,' said Joffo. He pulled up another chair and sat down. 'Today was the day you paraded down our little street once too often.'

My throat was dry, and there was a pounding in my temples. 'What is the meaning of this, monsieur?'

'Who are you? What do you want from us?'

I tried to sit up straight despite my bonds. 'What are you talking about?'

The barber felt my pockets. His nose cast a heavy shadow over his mouth. Finding nothing, he drew his hand back. 'Where are your papers?'

In that moment, I saw myself the way I had seen others. Tied to a chair under a blinding light, and asked questions to which there were no answers.

'They got lost.'

'Who are you?'

'A Frenchman, like yourself.'

'A Frenchman and a collaborator,' the barber replied.

'Who says so?' Angrily, I shifted myself forward.

'Who are the people you're in contact with? Vichy? Gestapo?'

I considered my answer. The truth was worse than either of them guessed. I wasn't collaborating; I was the real thing. I was the most complete and immediate witness to the interrogations, the first to learn everything the SS wanted to know. When I stopped and thought about it, I realized that at that moment I was face-to-face with the *enemy*. Thought fragments flashed through my head. Communist workers, courageous priests, and veterans of the first war belonged to the Resistance. There were duplicating machines in cellars. Slogans scrawled on house walls and palisade fences. Some woman on the cleaning staff had smuggled information out of Transport Command. There was the boy who stole the carburetors in order to cripple a prisoner transport. Mostly isolated cases. There didn't appear to be any organization or any hierarchy, just a few weapons. Was *this* the adversary that Leibold and his team feared and fought against with all their might? An old bookseller and a bad-tempered barber?

'How did your papers get lost?'

'A raid. The Germans,' I replied.

'You're an informer,' the bookseller declared, shaking his head.

I looked at him indignantly. 'Don't informers always have the best papers?'

Joffo smoothed his bushy beard. 'Tell me what happened to your passport.'

I searched my memory of the interrogations in rue des Saussaies. When was Leibold most likely to believe his prisoners? When they gave up and whimpered, or when they grew outraged and rebellious? I looked Joffo straight in the eyes.

'They stopped the Paris train,' I said sullenly.

'Where?'

'A little before Thiers. Supposedly, the tracks were cut. Everyone had to get off. The soldiers took away my ID. To verify it, they said. I never got it back.'

'What kind of soldiers?'

'The ones with the death's head.' I didn't take my eyes off the bookseller.

'Why should the SS take an interest in you, of all people?' The barber stepped closer to me.

'Haven't got a clue. They held me for two days.'

'In which prison?' The old fellow's eyes, his boar's eyes, scrutinized me attentively.

'No prison. A *Lager*. A camp in the woods.'

Details—camp lists, deportation plans, sabotage reports—churned around in my head. I examined everything to see what would fit into my story.

'On the third day, I heard an officer say we were going to be put in a transport convoy.' I struggled against the ropes. 'But I had no desire to be dragged off to Germany to make artillery shells.'

'You escaped?' the barber asked in disbelief.

Joffo bent forward. 'How?'

'We were supposed to be taken to a transit camp south of Moulins. On the way, the tracks went up a steep hill. The train slowed down, and I jumped out.' I lowered my head.

Silence. I felt the two of them look at each other. 'Hmm,' said Joffo. 'None of this can be verified.'

The barber planted himself in front of me. 'We can make you tell us the truth!'

In my mind's eye, I saw the tub full of water, the broken limbs, the corporals striking blow after blow. The threat sounded phony. The small-boned fellow didn't look as though he'd had much experience in hitting people.

The old man sat down and made himself comfortable. 'You're staying here until you tell us everything we want to know.'

That was impossible: I had to be out of there by midnight. A corporal who didn't make it back to his quarters by lights-out could get away with a reprimand. But not showing up for duty in rue des Saussaies would be no trifling matter.

'What about the apartment you stay in?' Joffo asked. 'The place in the second arrondissement.'

This revelation was like a blow. Chantal! Clearly, she'd reported on me to her father. No, not to her father—to her cell leader. In a flash, I understood; I realized that it was *Chantal* who had struck up a conversation with *me.* She'd lulled me into a sense of security with the *Fables.* She'd gone out with me for a whole evening, raising my hopes. I cursed my vanity, cursed myself, for letting her take me in like that.

'The apartment,' Joffo repeated.

I thought about the key in my pocket. If they searched me more thoroughly, they'd find it.

'Belongs to a friend,' I replied.

'Is he an informer, too?' the barber asked.

In a split second, I remembered Hirschbiegel's mentioning a proxy. His name?

I laughed. 'You think someone named *Isaak Wasserlof*'s an informer for the Germans?'

'He's a Jew?' The barber was astounded.

They held a brief whispered powwow.

'If you live in the second,' Joffo said, 'why are you in this neighbourhood so often?'

'You should be able to figure out the answer to that.' My smile was not a success.

'Chantal?' her father asked. 'But why her? There are thousands of other girls.'

I shrugged my shoulders. 'I don't know, either, monsieur.'

The barber butted in. 'I don't believe you're sniffing around here just on account of Chantal,' he said. 'Where do you come from?'

I invented names. Parents, grandparents. I described the streets of my childhood and evoked my friendship with Wasserlof, who'd invited me to stay with him in Paris. In the hope that the Sorbonne would start holding classes again, I said, I'd come to register for the fall semester. But then my papers had been taken away, and . . .

'Have you applied for new papers?' the barber asked. 'Show us the thing they give you, the confirmation.'

I laughed harshly. 'Have you got any idea how many hours I've spent standing in the application line? And I've never once reached the front of it.'

Remarkably, they seemed to believe that one. Typical German harassment. Having to wait days and weeks in the halls of the records office for a new 'certificate' that would never be issued: This was the Parisian reality. For a moment, they were ready to believe they were dealing with a young Frenchman who'd fallen in love with the bookseller's daughter. Taking advantage of the mood swing, I asked Joffo to untie me. He examined my swollen wrists and gave a sign to the barber, who stepped behind me and began to undo the cords.

'How do you make a living?' the old man asked.

'I manage to get by.'

He tilted his head to one side. 'You recently paid for something with a large bill.'

I felt the knots loosening. 'Wasserlof gave me some money.'

'The bill was freshly printed.' Joffo's voice sounded more suspicious.

My hands were almost free. 'So what?'

'I didn't know about the money,' the barber said.

I stood up and took a step toward the stairs.

'Just a minute, my friend!' All of a sudden, I was gazing down the barrel of an army pistol. I reached the bottom stair in one bound, throwing off the rope as I moved.

'Halt!'

I ran up the stairs without looking back. Above my head, the dark rectangle, outlined in light. I raised the trapdoor with my shoulders. Felt something strike my leg and, simultaneously, heard a shot. Although the impact almost knocked me down, I scrambled up through the opening, heaving the trapdoor aside. It struck the floor with a crash. I was in the stockroom; the barber's head emerged behind me.

'Freeze!'

'I've told you everything!'

Another shot rang out. The bullet struck some books near me. I dashed into the shop, jumped behind some bookshelves, and crept toward the door. The barber took aim at me from behind the counter. Still crouching, I tore the door open; the bell sounded. The last time I looked, the bookseller was pushing down the barber's hand.

'Not here,' Joffo said.

I ran out and sprang down the steps. I sprinted past the big rock and down rue de Gaspard, noticed the surprised look on the junk dealer's face, opened the black gate, and reached the street, the boulevard, on the other side. Once I was among the crowd, my breathing grew calmer. I passed the Lubinsky slowly. On the Pont Royal, I looked around. There didn't seem to be anyone following me.

It was getting dark. Only then did I notice that it hurt to walk. A dark spot on my trouser leg, gradually spreading. The bullet had ripped a chunk of flesh out of my calf. I reached the ruined building, tore my shirt into strips, and bound up my wound. Then I put my checkered suit, my soft shoes, and my hat in the laundry bag and closed it up as though I never wanted to open it again.

Roth, Wehrmacht soldier, summer 1943. On my way back to the hotel, I thought, the fellow has a nationality. In which he consists. The grey uniform, the hooked cross, the flag. As long as the war lasted, those things were my reality. Oddly relieved to have come through my adventure practically in one piece, I limped back to the hotel, dropped off my bag in my room, and went upstairs to see Hirschbiegel. I intended to propose

73

something to the lieutenant: a fun-filled boys' night out. Two Germans in enemy territory.

11

Two weeks later, just before I went on duty, Leibold met me in the hall.

'I was right!' He appeared to be in unusually good humour as he pushed back his cap and rubbed his shiny pate. 'The Gascon has led us to his rat hole.'

Only now did it occur to me that I hadn't seen the offender's face for days. I remembered the amazing patience Leibold had shown while interrogating this man, without obtaining any worthwhile result. Hunkered down like a mossy stone, the Gascon made his stolid denials; even the corporals' *techniques* made no impression on him.

'I let him go,' Leibold said affably, 'and that's where he went. It's a shop we've had our eyes on for a long time. A barbershop.'

For a moment, I had the feeling that the dead-level floor in front of me was sloping downward. Leibold walked on, thereby forcing me to accompany him.

'Our friend thinks he's clever,' he said with a big smile. 'He got a haircut, paid, and left. Shortly afterward, he sneaked back in through a neighbouring house.'

An unexpected ray of light struck me; outside, it was a most gorgeous day.

'And have you already . . . taken action?'

'There's no hurry.' We reached the orderly

74

room. 'My people are watching everyone who goes in or out of the shop. In a few days, we'll strike.' Leibold grabbed the door handle. 'And then, the barber's going to get a very close shave!'

'And where is this shop?' I asked a touch too hastily.

'In the sixth, close to the river.' Leibold turned around. 'Do you know the area?'

I pretended to give this question some thought. Without waiting for my answer, he disappeared into his room.

Staring at the scuffed stone floor, I noticed a first lieutenant too late and saluted when he was already past me. Slowly, I took off my forage cap and clamped my case under my arm. A PFC snatched the office door open right in front of me and nearly ran me down. I stepped in and said, 'Good morning.' A mumbled 'Morning' from every table. I took out my writing pad and sharpened my pencil. Rieleck-Sostmann gave me a provocative look. There was something different about her. Her hair was gathered into artificial curls on the sides of her head. French girls had recently started wearing their hair like this, but it wasn't a look that suited a tall German woman. I nodded, acknowledging her coiffure, and she smiled at me and patted her new curls. Without exchanging a word with her, I kept moving, crossed the room, and sat down at my little table. The corporals were sweating already, and they hadn't even gone into action yet. I watched Leibold's booted legs walk past me with measured steps. I couldn't bring myself to look any of the culprits in the eye.

*   *   *

75

During the midday break, Anna Rieleck-Sostmann joined me and ate her black-bread sandwich. 'So how are your French promenades going?' she asked.

I sat there with my eyes closed, as though enjoying the sun. 'I've given them up,' I replied quite truthfully.

'No more rambling?'

It was impossible not to think about Chantal. Her cheerfully bobbing walk as she hurried through the narrow streets ahead of me. The last look she gave me before I marched into the trap. The way she smelled the one time she opened her lips for me.

That evening, I lay in Rieleck-Sostmann's energetic arms and touched Chantal at the same time. Frau R. noticed the difference and spurred on my despairing passion. She grew so loud in this endeavour that my telephoning neighbour pounded on the wall. I wasn't able to hold on to Chantal for very long. I was left alone with Rieleck-Sostmann. She cut up a strudel someone had sent her from the Reich. I lay on my back, chewing the raisins, and watched the big girl get dressed. One floor above us, the gramophone began to play. I moved my lips to the words of 'Ma Pomme' and smiled at the realization that Hirschbiegel was now my only ray of hope. The fat lieutenant with the childish conception of women had become my friend.

'What are you smiling about?' Rieleck-Sostmann was tightening her garter straps.

'Your new hairdo looks good.' I looked away.

After she left, I went upstairs to visit the

lieutenant. In the hall, my neighbour from the next room looked at me respectfully.

Hirschbiegel was already out of his bath. 'Tonight's the night,' he said, beaming. 'My luck's about to change. You'll see!' He held his breath and buttoned his pants.

The cognac was warm. Hirschbiegel added some cold water to it, and we drank.

'Tell me what you think about my latest treasure.' He proudly picked up a brown record sleeve from the table and extracted a gleaming disk. 'Bought it yesterday!' He set his machine in motion and placed the record on the turntable.

'So now you've doubled your collection,' I said with a smile. 'What's this?'

A musette band played café music. I poured myself some more cognac and made myself comfortable on Hirschbiegel's bed.

Maurice Chevalier sang about a girl he fell in love with in April; in the summer, he left her for someone else. The girl was sad, but Chevalier consoled her. She'd be his April girl. He'd come back next year. *'Avril prochain—je reviens!'*

'What will next April be like?' I said.

We listened to the rest of the song in silence.

When we left the hotel, Hirschbiegel smelled of violet water and had tamed his curls with brilliantine. 'Let's paint the town,' he said, his face full of hope.

We strolled toward the Seine, had a meal in a riverside restaurant, and walked west along the bank. The rear view of a buxom flower girl attracted the lieutenant's interest; we followed her for two bridges. He bought one of her little bouquets but didn't have the nerve to make her any further offer. Flowers in hand, he came back to me.

'At least it's a start,' he said shyly.

A soft evening; summer was already on the wane. You couldn't see it fading anywhere yet, but you could feel it. The heat had rolled up the chestnut leaves. In the overgrown gardens that sloped down to the river, women were at work, bent over or on their knees, tending potato plants, pulling up weeds and burning them. Stinging nettles overran the meagre, narrow flower beds on the bank. There was a baby carriage in the shade of a tree, and next to it the child's mother huddled, dressed in black; another woman was cutting grass with a sickle. A worker glided past on a clattering bicycle. Tree limbs, thick as arms and marked with fresh axe cuts, were tied to his handlebars, forming a swaying bundle that stuck out like spears for several feet on either side. I watched my shadow creep along ahead of me with slumping shoulders.

'So look, buddy, what's wrong?' The lieutenant stood in my way.

'What could be wrong? It's hot.' I fixed my eyes on the shadow.

'You're the picture of misery, do you know that?' He furrowed his brow and looked worried. 'Come on, tell me what's bothering you.'

I tried to get around him by moving toward the river. 'Nothing,' I said. 'Nothing at all.'

'Is it the death's-head boys?' He stumbled along beside me. 'And the prisoners, right? Is all that getting to you?'

I wiped my hand across my forehead. Things were very busy in rue des Saussaies. The interrogations had multiplied by leaps and bounds.

Executions were more frequent. The prisons were bursting at the seams. New camps had been set up. Shots rang out in the night. Leibold, under pressure, was becoming grimmer. He allowed the corporals to hold their 'physical education classes' more and more often. The marble building was swarming with Gestapo. Leaves were being cancelled. The general nervousness seemed to be growing with each passing day. But that wasn't it.

To change the subject, I asked Hirschbiegel, 'Is your unit supposed to move out?'

He nodded. 'We're waiting for marching orders from one hour to the next. They won't affect me. The colonel owes me about a thousand from bridge. He wants to win his money back.' At this point, words failed him, and so the lieutenant poked me in the side. 'Say, come on, now . . . I don't like it when you're down in the dumps. You lead a charmed life.'

Surprised, I looked my good-natured companion up and down. There were patches of sweat all over his uniform jacket; the massive fellow was positively streaming. 'Guys like you get all the breaks,' he said. 'You're a lucky stiff, Roth. Don't you know that?'

I sighed. 'But what's going to happen?' I replied softly.

'A woman?' He laughed out loud. 'I would never have guessed! The ladies' darling has it bad for someone? Who? A Frenchwoman?'

I nodded.

'Married?'

'Worse.'

'Nothing's worse.'

'She thinks I'm a swine.'

'You?' He stopped short. 'Then she doesn't deserve you. Or did you try something disgusting?'

I said nothing. The pounding in my temples came back.

'What went on with you two?' Hirschbiegel insisted.

'I pretended to be a Frenchman.'

I searched his eyes carefully; I had put myself in his hands. What I'd done was so outlandish that I had to explain it in exhaustive detail before Hirschbiegel could understand it. In the ensuing silence, we ducked under the arches of a bridge.

'Do you know you could be shot for that?' he blurted out. He braced his hands against his hips.

'First something happens,' I murmured. 'Some random thing. Then the next thing happens. And then the next.' My words rang hollow under the damp vaults. 'One thing after another, deeper and deeper.'

The stones reflected the movements of the water.

'Do you love her?'

I looked for a hint of irony in his face. 'These aren't the times for love.'

'What can you do, then?' He licked the salt from his upper lip.

'At best, you can focus on the next day,' I said. 'Every time you tear a page off the calendar, that's another victory.'

'Will you see her again?'

'As what? As a Frenchman, a German, an SS translator?'

'As you,' Hirschbiegel replied.

'There's nothing to be done.' I shivered in the shade. 'I tear off calendar pages.'

80

'And I play bridge,' the fat lieutenant said. 'It's a strange war.'

We walked on. I listened to our footsteps, sounding in unison. We took the next steps leading up from the riverbank and climbed back to the street.

12

I put on the better uniform and considered myself in the mirror as I straightened my belt. The Wehrmacht corporal, a young man with anxious eyes.

I wasn't doing it out of concern, which is what I'd told myself at first. I wasn't doing it to protect myself against possible discovery. I was doing it so I could see her again.

Slowly and thoughtfully, I had something to eat in a little restaurant around the corner. Uncharacteristically, I drank three glasses of red wine with my meal. Then I set out on my walk. I went a few blocks beyond the avenue de l'Opéra and passed the open area the Wehrmacht used as a parking lot. The pasty-white sentry posted in front of army headquarters had a damp forehead and seemed about to keel over on the spot. I turned north. The soot from the old chimneys was being washed into the gutters. A beanpole SS lieutenant bent down toward his companion, a listless blond woman. Three Silesian PFCs wearing badly fitting uniforms conversed in their thick dialect. Probably reservists, I thought. You saw more and more of them in the city; the combat troops were disappearing eastward. The men's arms were full of packages, so much so that they were unable to salute a passing captain with anything but their eyes. Next came two promenading Parisian ladies; their faces looked hollow, their lips and cheeks sucked in. They patted their hairdos nervously as I passed by.

I was getting close to the Trinité square. It was after hours in the pastry shop, but the line of customers waiting to get in had kept the place from closing on time. In their midst stood an officer from the municipal administration, who, it seemed, had broken into line; several small women assailed him. Meanwhile, the rolling shutters came down, and the CLOSED sign was displayed. The officer went off grumbling, as did the housewives. Posters announced guest performances in Paris by the Berlin State Opera. On the posters, a prima donna's dazzling white face and a bouquet of flowers. When I neared the Pigalle quarter, I thought I needed to rest. Actually, I wanted to give my anxiety a little time. I went into a bar and ordered a glass of absinthe. As I drank, I grasped my uniform sleeve with my free hand, as though trying to touch my current existence, my present. I paid and left.

Now I was only a few streets away. Between the buildings came the muffled sound of thunder burrowing behind the clouds. It wouldn't rain tonight. I passed the Scheherazade. The doorman made an enticing gesture, but I didn't slow down.

And there was Turachevsky's, looking deserted and unreal. I came to a stop a few metres from the door. My collar was too tight; my forehead was sweaty. A group of privates pushed past, cheerfully inviting me to join their party. I stepped to the door with them. Madame herself let us in.

'You're rather early, gentlemen,' she said with a professional smile.

A swarm of girls and women charged the sofas and settees. They wore simple white smocks—the kimonos would appear after midnight, when the officers were there. I stuck my forage cap under my epaulet and looked around.

'And you, my son?' Madame's fan whirled. 'We've met before, *n'est-ce pas?* You prefer—let me guess.' She liked to keep business moving along briskly; indecisive customers slowed down her turnover.

I anticipated her recommendation and disappeared into the bar, where I ordered an absinthe and sat at one of the farther tables. The tenor stepped onto the stage, surrounded by ladies in evening dress. He sang about the 'little difference.' The soldiers started clapping for the dance show. The atmosphere was lighter and freer than it had been the night I was there with the officers. This group drank the less expensive booze, but in great quantities; many guys needed to get their courage up before venturing into the salon.

The girls danced to the strains of the invincibly popular 'Ma Pomme': one step left, three steps right, howls from the blond audience. The piano player struggled with the tempo. Confusion among the dancers, girlish legs moving in disaccord. The little orchestra played stubbornly on.

How mellow it is in here, I thought. Letting the green spirit take effect, I opened a button or two on my uniform and observed my fingers as they beat time to the music. The fear was still there, but masked. I was waiting for whatever came next.

Some half-naked girls used a dwarf as a watering can. The little fellow cried out in a croaking voice, 'Water the vegetables! Don't let my little flowers dry up!' Laughter. A man with performing pigeons induced the pampered birds to jump through hoops and pull a pretty little wagon. He was shouted off the stage when his artistes shit on his evening coat. The rubber man picked up a harmonica with his feet and played a German march.

The dancers appeared in innumerable costumes, ten girls at a time; Chantal was never among them. I was suspended in a green fog. The reason for my visit had fled into other spheres. I watched the piano player and admired his ability to accompany whatever was happening on the stage and make his way flawlessly through all the current hits. He was a man in his fifties. I imagined his life. Studies at the conservatoire, interrupted from 1914 to 1918 by the war. Afterward, concerts in small towns and marriage to a singer, who sacrificed her career for their children; his playing kept the family afloat. Cabarets, barrooms, and finally this whorehouse in Pigalle. He was paid by the hour. The more tunes he banged out, the more money he took home. Sometimes a plastered major stuck a hundred-franc note into his pocket so that he would play 'Schön Rosmarin' or 'Lippen Schweigen.'

Chantal came on as a sultan's favorite wife. The other girls wore black wigs; holding little cymbals, they gathered in a circle around Chantal. She tossed back her own real hair and greeted the sultan. Frivolous laughter started to well up inside

84

me. The pianist was playing chords in fifths that sounded more Chinese than Arabic. The stage pasha had Chantal dance the Dance of the Veils while the other girls obsequiously offered themselves to him. When the last bit of fabric had fallen, Chantal left the stage. The soldiers applauded. I tore through my own veil and stood up. With no more thought for the danger I'd been brooding over for hours, I stumbled in the general direction of the band.

'*Accès interdit, monsieur,*' the piano player called out without interrupting the flow of his harem music. Turning my head, I gave him a glassy smile, disappeared behind the velvet border, and collided with the tenor. In the harsh glare of a spotlight, I could see that he was an old man. Watery eyes looked me up and down; white hair peeked out from under his pitch-black wig.

'Ready for a duet, soldier?' His lips were painted so as to make his mouth look like a little heart. Thick powder masked a skin rash, and a scarf covered his wrinkled neck. I pushed him aside and stumbled into the narrow passage. My hobnailed boots made considerable noise.

'*Vous allez où, m'sieur?*' As he spoke, the stage manager moved a control on the light board and a garish violet shimmer was reflected from the stage.

'Chantal,' I said hoarsely, and left the man behind me.

Bluish light in the corridor. Scraps of words and laughter from behind closed doors. I stood there, reeling and helpless. From the stage, the strains of the 'Toreador Song.' I called Chantal. The conversations fell silent for a moment and then began again. Finale and flourish; feeble applause.

85

'Come out here, Chantal!' The weight of my own voice sent me staggering against a paper wall, which began to move. Dancing girls flitted past; some ran into me. Brief curses.

The sultan appeared before me. *'Quittez la scène, les boches!'* A muscular forearm crushed itself against the back of my neck, forcing me to bend down.

'Georges, t'es fou?' The girls, practically naked, grabbed the patriot from behind and pulled him back. The grip on my neck disappeared; the women gathered around me. *'Tout va bien, monsieur. Vous vous amusez? On peut aider?'*

I gasped for air. 'Chantal!'

Whispering around me: *'Qu'est-ce qu'il veut? Ça vous dit quelque chose, Chantal?'* In the background, the tenor began the song about his Froufrou's faithlessness. The girls swore. *'Léonard a déjà commencé. Putain!'* They left me standing there, threw on another bit of fabric as they ran, and bounded onto the stage.

At the end of the corridor, I reached a door. It hung askew, hinges squealing, and opened outward onto an inner courtyard, overgrown with ivy and lighted by the summer moon. Chimney-high walls on every side, and crouched in a corner, Chantal. I leaned against the door frame; she looked up. It took her several seconds to process the combination of my face and my uniform. Then she sprang to her feet, deeply shocked, quivering from head to toe. She had covered herself with a faded dressing gown. The summer breeze played with her hair.

'Chantal.' After all the opening lines I'd come up with, this was the only word that occurred to

86

me. I started to go over to her. My boot heels made a sharp sound on the worn, shiny threshold. 'I want to warn you.'

'Devil,' she said in a low voice, snatching together the lapels of her dressing gown. 'You devil.'

'I've been looking for you, Chantal.' She tried to dash past me, but the courtyard was small, and I was able to spring to the side and catch her arm. She turned around, stepped close to me, and spat. The absinthe made me sluggish and strong. She didn't get away.

'Chantal, listen to me!' I shouted. It came out in German.

'German pig! Let me go!'

She struck me in the face as hard as she could; the following blow landed very low on my abdomen. I staggered and crashed into the wall. In one bound, she was through the door. The old wood splintered as it slammed behind her. I followed, my elbows pressed against my belly.

'I have to warn you, Chantal!'

A door opposite me opened a crack. When the dwarf saw my uniform, he quickly drew back. Darkness in the corridor. My footsteps hammered the floor as I went after her. I followed her all through the backstage labyrinth at Turachevsky's. Once, I saw the tail of her gown disappearing around a corner. Astonished performers jumped aside; cigarette-smoking girls in kimonos pressed themselves against the wall.

At last, the salon opened out in front of me. I stumbled over the edge of the carpet, lost my balance, and fell to the floor under the chandelier. The women on the sofas giggled. Madame

87

entered. Before I could explain it all to her, a pair of boots appeared in front of me. As my eyes wandered upward, I recognized the second lieutenant's face. He laughed his familiar bleating laugh. Behind him, the colonel interrupted his concentration on lighting his cigar to cast a surprised glance in my direction. I got to my feet quickly, unsteadily. The green fairy had flown away. I came to attention.

'Stand at ease,' the colonel growled. 'We're not on the drill field.' His face softened into a fleshy grin. 'The kids are playing hide-and-seek in here,' he said. The second lieutenant giggled.

My eyes looked feverishly for Chantal. Innumerable doors, a curtain in front of a passageway. Steps leading somewhere.

His cigar successfully lighted, the colonel paid no more attention to me. He and his retinue disappeared into the bar. I stood under the chandelier and started feeling sick. Very slowly, exaggeratedly slowly, I pulled my forage cap out of my epaulet and put it on my head. Madame's farewell sounded from far away. I stepped into the night air.

I'd made everything worse. Chantal's suspicion was now a certainty: I was the enemy, the German pig. I could do nothing more for her. I set out at a half trot across the square. The green fairy had left behind a dark, burning sensation; I needed water. Back in my hotel room, I drank from the tap greedily, like an ox. Bright moonlit night; dreamless sleep. I kept my boots on.

13

August was hot. The order of the day in rue des Saussaies granted shirtsleeve privileges. Leibold did not allow himself this convenience. Uniform jacket, belt buckle, Merit Cross snug against his throat. He gave the impression of someone who always felt cold.

'Today,' he said.

Days had passed since we'd last had a smoke together by the window. Down in the garden, the wilting grass was knee-high. No one did anything about it. I missed the one-armed gardener.

'Today, I have an appointment at the barber's,' Leibold said with a thin smile. 'We seem to be dealing with a pretty large cell.'

'The barbershop?' I considered the plane tree, whose leaves were turning red.

He nodded and said, 'Rue Jacob.' I stared at the point in the window where the mullion crossed the transom. The cross dissolved in the sunlight. 'Do you know this shop?'

I cleared my throat. 'I'm sure I've passed it a time or two.'

He moved closer. 'After this evening, it won't exist anymore.'

I took the cigarette he offered. He waited until the first cloud of smoke had ascended above us before continuing. 'The Gascon will be there. Turning out pamphlets, probably. We figure the machine's in the cellar.'

'A night operation?' I asked.

'Not necessarily.' Leibold shook his head. 'The

Parisians have to see how far we're willing to go.'
He held his cigarette perpendicular to the floor,
balancing the ash. 'You'll probably have a lot of
work to do tomorrow.'

'I understand, Captain.'

'Are you feeling well?' His face came nearer.

'How do you mean?' I straightened my spine.

'Of late, you haven't been all there, my friend.
I've noticed it for a while now.'

I was startled. Inconspicuous, appropriate—
that's what I wanted to be. I didn't want anyone
focusing on me. 'Hasn't my performance been—'

'It's not work-related,' he said, waving
dismissively. Ashes fell on his sleeve. 'Tell me, man
to man: What's eating you?'

'Nothing, Herr Leibold—that is, Captain.' I
came to attention. 'I'll try harder from now on, sir.'

'You're a hard fellow to figure out, Corporal,'
the bald man said. 'Can I help you in some way?' I
could feel his sincerity, and I knew how dangerous
such sympathy was. 'Take the afternoon off.'
Leibold threw down his cigarette and ground it out
under his heel. No privilege, I thought. Normality.
Distance. 'Rest and relax,' he said. 'Why not
go swimming? It'll probably be your last chance
this year.' He wiped his skull with a white
handkerchief. I clicked my heels together too late
and watched the black uniform disappear at the
end of the hall.

*   *   *

No sound from anywhere. The hotel appeared
deserted. Nobody walking down the corridors,
nobody making a phone call. Everyone was on

duty somewhere else. Except me, there alone, lying on my bed and listening. Faint traffic noise. A single drip in the bathroom. I felt like the only living creature in the building. With every minute that I lost, the possibility of doing anything grew smaller. But my chances of survival increased. I had to make a decision; I had to act. I remained where I was—on my back. I shoved a pillow under my head and gazed at the shepherd girls. The curtain's grey-green reminded me of Chantal's eyes.

I sat up as though I had just awakened. Averting my eyes from the mirror, I opened the wardrobe and bent down to the cloth bag. I stayed like that for several seconds and then, finally, I seized the handle and swung the bag onto the bed. Then I turned slowly toward the wall. The calendar was hanging there; today's date hadn't been torn off yet. I'll do it later tonight, I thought, after I get back. When I felt the material of my checkered suit between my fingers, everything stood still.

Nothing was different. The facade of the condemned building hung dangerously far out over the sidewalk. The coolness of the entryway welcomed me. I took off my uniform more carefully than usual and meticulously folded the shirt and the trousers. After cramming the shafts of my boots into the laundry bag, I took off my ID tags and weighed the little chain in my hand. With incomprehensible reverence, I slipped the tags back over my head and felt the metal on my chest. I quickly buttoned my civilian shirt up to my neck.

This evening, Monsieur Antoine was a self under duress. I was playing a role. I hurried through the streets, my eyes on the pavement. The way seemed longer than before. Suspicious silence on the Pont Royal. Why did the soldiers on the bridge stare at me? I didn't take my usual route along the boulevard; instead, I sidled down narrow alleys and slipped through solitary passageways, approaching rue Jacob by detours.

The waiter at the Lubinsky invited me to have a seat. I didn't slow down. Step by step, the café disappeared behind me. Two sergeants came around the corner; I hugged the wall and continued on. Finally, I reached the Jewish haberdasher's shop. The barber's windows glimmered just beyond it. Alert and apprehensive, I scouted around. Was the task force already lurking somewhere? Had Leibold sent assault troops or men in civilian clothes? Were they posted in the entryways of the neighbouring buildings, their eyes fixed on the barbershop?

If I walk past the salon now, I thought, and reach the next corner and return to my field grey reality, it will be as if none of this ever happened. I'll tear the page off the calendar, just as I do every day. But if I stop and open this door, I'll have nothing in front of me and nothing behind me except the abyss.

The brass door handle. The tinkling of the shop bell.

'*Bonjour, monsieur.* You won't have long to wait.'

As always, the old man was there, reading his newspaper. A customer sat in the broad-backed chair, her wet hair combed down over her face. Chantal stood at the cash register. At that moment, the sun disappeared behind an isolated cloud. The barber turned around.

No one said anything.

92

I began. In my very best French.

'Once upon a time, there was an animal. It had the head of a bear, but its hindquarters resembled a zebra's. When people saw it from the front, they said, 'That's a bear.' The people who observed the beast from behind declared it was a zebra. And because no one saw it from both the back and the front at once, a quarrel arose. The animal didn't understand what the argument was about, because it experienced itself as a single whole.'

I spoke the last sentence in Chantal's direction. Her eyes were dark with confusion. She braced herself with both hands on the cash drawer.

'What's he talking about?' the barber hissed. 'What does he want?'

During my tale, the customer had parted her hair like a curtain and looked at me in the mirror.

'Close your shop, monsieur,' I said to the barber. 'Immediately would be best.'

'Are you mad?' He came closer to me.

'You have to leave.' I turned in the direction of the cashier's desk. 'You, too, Chantal.'

'What do *you* know about this?' the barber asked her fiercely.

'Nothing.' She didn't move an inch.

Suddenly, and for the first time since I'd entered the shop, the old man lowered his newspaper. I could see white hair and glittering blue eyes. He looked me up and down.

'Are you the *boche*?' he asked.

'Yes, I'm the *boche*.'

Calmly, the old man rested his hands on his newspaper. 'And you're the zebra, and you're also the bear?'

'Just so, monsieur.'

93

The old man turned to the barber. 'Listen to him, Gustave.' As he said this, he folded the paper and stood up.

'Why should I, Papa?'

'Do it.' The old man took his hat from the hook, opened the door, and stepped out. He seemed to be checking the weather. Then, after lingering in the sun for a few moments, he finally began strolling down rue Jacob.

'Let's go in the back.' Gustave pointed to a glass-bead curtain. 'We'll just be a second, madame,' he said, turning briefly to the customer, who watched in amazement as he withdrew.

I stepped through the strings of beads; Chantal was the last to enter. A tiny kitchen, a small round table. The barber pointed me to the only chair. Chantal leaned on the sink. The glass beads were still clicking.

After a brief silence, I said, 'You're waiting for the Gascon.'

The barber exchanged glances with Chantal. 'Who?'

I described the man.

'We don't know him.'

'I translated his interrogation,' I said. 'They set him free. And now he's led them to you. When is he coming?'

Despite the tense silence and their mutual consternation, I couldn't help looking at Chantal. She was breathing hard, her breasts rising and falling.

'We're not waiting for anybody,' the barber said, lying.

'At six-thirty,' said Chantal, interrupting him. He stared at her.

'Six-thirty,' I repeated, remembering the clocks striking six just after I crossed the bridge. 'Then there's hardly any time.'

I held my clenched fists between my knees and told my story as calmly as I could, addressing most of it to Chantal. The beaded curtain broke up the light coming into the room.

'That's quite a tale you tell,' the barber said brusquely.

'Why are you doing this?' Chantal pushed a lock of her hair behind her ear. 'Those are your people.'

I shrugged my shoulders. 'What good will it do if you all get arrested?'

Suddenly, the barber sprang to the little passageway and peeked out between the strings of beads. In the late-afternoon light, you could see the nose of an automobile that was pulling up in front of the shop window. A second car approached from the left. These vehicles weren't marked in any way, but the locals knew them well.

Gustave whipped around. 'This is a trap!' He stood very close to me.

I rose from my chair. 'In that case, I wouldn't have needed to say anything!'

The shop bell rang in the next room. The woman with wet hair hastily left the salon and ran past the uniformed men who were getting out of the cars. One of them checked her papers.

'Get out of here!' I hissed.

Chantal nodded to Gustave. Outside the door of the shop, the men were receiving orders from a sergeant. The barber started frantically shoving aside some boxes that concealed a low door.

'What will happen to you?' Chantal asked me as

95

the barber unbolted the door.

'If they catch me, they'll treat me the same as you.'

She struggled with herself for a second and then pointed into the unlighted passageway on the other side of the little door. I stooped. The barber hurried ahead of me. Chantal came last.

We went through a narrow corridor, then up some steps into a cellar. The barber opened a grille. I smelled wine and resinous wine barrels. We came to a storeroom. A ray of light fell from a shaft that opened in the courtyard above our heads. The barber led the way to a spiral staircase. Chantal gathered up her skirt so she'd be able to run better. We reached a corridor at ground level. *'Attention!'* A whispered cry came from the depths of a flat. Electric lightbulb, under it a silhouette. The barber stopped before entering an inner courtyard. I noticed some people on balconies, eyeing us curiously. Chantal caught up with us; I felt her breath on my back. A woman scolded her child. A radio: the German broadcast to France. More keys, then another passage, and at its far end we could see the street. We had crossed the entire square block, from one side to the other. The barber headed for the archway.

Chantal called out, 'Your jacket!'

He fumbled with buttons and flung the white smock away.

'Wait!' I peered outside. I knew their tactics. First came the uniforms, chasing the fox out of his lair. Behind them, men in civilian clothes lay in wait. I stuck my head out past the projecting brick facade. Red afternoon sun, street noise, normality. There was a car parked on the opposite side of the

96

street, near it another one with its engine running, both French models. A man stood next to the first car and smoked a cigarette. Gray suit, inconspicuous tie. I narrowed my eyes. Despite the dusty day, his shoes were perfectly polished. I drew back.

'They're outside,' I whispered. 'Is there another way out?'

Chantal turned around and faced the courtyard. 'The cellar,' she said. 'But that means we have to go back.'

'No. We'll run!' The barber dug his fists into his pockets.

'In these shoes?' Chantal said, pointing to her heels.

I looked at Gustave. 'They've got people posted on every corner.'

Shouts, slamming doors. The moment had passed. Boots battered against an obstacle. The barber took two steps forward, two steps back, gnawing the backs of his hands. The first salvos of gunfire; a lock burst. Shouts of protest, German replies. Somewhere a child was crying.

Gustave moved closer to the light. 'Let's split up, then.'

Chantal nodded. 'Good luck.'

He shot out of the dark entrance, darted sideways, and dashed away. The man with the polished shoes immediately jumped into the car. Dark suits appeared from every direction. I watched them run past the archway, just a few metres away from us. Startled pedestrians stopped walking. A shot. The street froze. A man threw himself to the pavement. More shots, now farther off. Chantal listened with a finger on her lips.

97

Then no more sounds. Several long seconds passed. The street returned to its normal rhythm. The man on the pavement stood up and brushed off his pants. Someone honked at a bicycle rider, who rode past us, lurching from side to side. Two women pushed a cart.

'Now what?' Chantal was very close to me.

Voices behind us. Turmoil. Booted steps on the metal balustrades. We stood in the shadow of the projecting facade. Someone shouted from below in German, 'We've got the printing press!'

'They've found your press,' I said, translating.

'What shall we do?' Her head was moving from side to side.

'Chantal?' Our eyes met.

'Yes?'

'Can you laugh?' I took her hand.

'Laugh?' She pulled it back.

'The whole thing is just a giant joke.'

A young man in a checkered suit stepped out of the archway. Behind him came a pretty woman in a dress with blue stripes. She was laughing at the top of her voice. As he continued on, she caught his arm. He had to hold on to her, because she was doubled over with laughter.

'*Arrête. Ça suffit,*' he said.

'*Il a . . . il . . . il a jeté sa chaussure.*' She threw her head back, couldn't contain herself, laughed so hard that the street was filled with the sound of it. People everywhere turned to look.

'*Calme-toi. Ils regardent tous.*' The young man found her merriment distasteful.

'*La chaussure! Il a jeté sa chaussure!*' She held her sides. Snot and spat dribbled down her chin.

He grabbed her by the waist. '*Oui, sa chaussure,*

98

j'ai compris.'

The word sent her off into another cascade of laughter. Her reddish brown hair fell in her face.

He tried to make her walk on. *'Allons. Il est tard.'* He smiled at some passersby, imploring their understanding.

The strange couple passed a black automobile. Its occupants, two men wearing suits, had their windows rolled down. One of them stared after the two young people; the other was infected by the girl's laughter. 'They're having fun,' he said.

An empty troop carrier was parked at the next corner. An SS private leaned against the tailgate with his booted legs crossed and rolled himself a cigarette. 'Sounds like the young lady's swallowed some laughing gas,' he remarked with a smile.

The young man didn't understand. *'Pardon, monsieur?'*

The soldier spat out a few tobacco crumbs. 'Pretty, but nuts,' he said as the couple disappeared around a curve in the street. Gradually, the laughter died down.

I walked faster. 'Are they following us?' Chantal asked, turning around.

I stroked her hip. 'Which way now?'

'Right.'

'That'll take us back to rue Jacob.'

'Trust me.'

We reached rue de Seine. A black automobile came toward us, moving slowly, as though on the lookout. I recognized Leibold's staff car only after it was too late. Chantal felt me hesitate. Inside the vehicle were two silhouettes, both wearing peaked caps.

I pulled Chantal close to me, turned her toward

99

the street, and kissed her on the mouth. My hands slid over her shoulders and down her back. I grabbed the cheeks of her butt and held her tight. Have a look at that, I thought. Look at that behind! Chantal made a hissing sound.

The car was even with us, moving even more slowly. I lifted my head a little and saw Leibold's face in the outside mirror. My mouth was pressed against Chantal's lips as my eyes met the captain's. But no sign of recognition entered his gaze. He merely observed the scene. A young man was kissing a young French girl. Leibold's eyes lingered on mine for what seemed an eternity. Then they slid past. The car gradually pulled away down rue de Seine and disappeared behind a vegetable truck.

The street was full of people, standing in the shade and talking fast. Others hurried by. I kissed Chantal. We kissed each other. From a distance, a siren, the sound of marching boots, German words around the next corner. Noise slowly returned to the late-afternoon sidewalk.

14

Sheds and warehouses, awnings over entryways, daubs of paint on greasy chimneys. Red-wine drinkers, belching in an alley. We were walking into the stony bowels of Montmartre. In the shade on the north side, a vineyard, gas holders, long sheds. Trains whizzed into the depths of the earth; clouds of industrial smoke billowed skyward. The horizon was hidden in a powdery haze.

We hadn't spoken since those minutes in rue Jacob. The skirts of Chantal's dress, pale blue stripes, swung out as she walked beside me. I tried to forget Leibold's face.

She looked at me. 'Why did you do it?'

They were sitting around here and there, drinking. Dozens of Luftwaffe personnel, fitted out with photographic equipment. A soldier fed the sparrows, looking around proudly whenever a bird picked up a crumb and flew away.

'They're your own people,' Chantal said, pressing me for an answer.

'Yes.'

'Then why?'

'I don't know why.'

Murmurs hung in the treetops. A violinist presented himself in the entrance of the restaurant and slid his fiddle under his chin. We passed a fountain on the way. I rolled up my shirtsleeves and drank. I wiped my hands on my shirt and stared at Chantal. 'They're looking for your father, too,' I said. The sweaty tendon in her throat tempted me to touch her.

'He's safe tonight.' She looked back involuntarily. 'We're going to meet tomorrow ...' She stopped short.

I smiled. 'Don't say it. I'm the *boche.*'

'You're the *boche,*' she repeated.

We reached the big terrace, the end of our climb up the Butte de Montmartre. The white marble mountain range of Sacré-Coeur loomed above us. Hundreds of people were crowding the hill. At our feet, the city filled every corner of the visible world. Two sergeants poked the air, shouting to each other the names of the buildings they

101

recognized. One after another, Chantal and I laid our four hands on the railing. I could feel the reddening sun on the back of my neck.

'This flat,' Chantal said. 'Does it really exist?'

I hadn't thought about Hirschbiegel's apartment in a long time. He himself had never mentioned it again. Cautiously, I patted my chest—and felt the little key. All those weeks, I'd carried the thing in my pocket, and now I pulled it out in disbelief. It had a silvered head etched with tiny curlicues.

'It exists,' I said.

'The Jew's flat in the second arrondissement.' Chantal kept her eyes on the view.

'Where is that?' I asked. She pointed downward.

Hirschbiegel had mentioned the address only once. I was convinced the name of the street had slipped my mind, but then, effortlessly, it appeared: Faillard. Without hesitation, I said, 'Number twelve, rue Faillard.'

Chantal nodded, turned away, and collided with a corporal, who apologized without leering.

We went down the eastern side of the hill. As I walked, I clutched the key. What if the flat were stuffed with German junk? The Führer's picture, German canned goods, postcards from Heidelberg?

The street ended in rue Clignancourt. What had looked like an unending labyrinth from above turned out to be, with some effort, negotiable. We reached rue La Fayette; we plunged into the chaos of rue Saint-Denis. Chantal didn't once ask for directions. Antoine accompanies the bookseller's daughter to the lieutenant's flat, I thought.

At the boundary of the second arrondissement, they'd set up a barricade, and they were driving the people out of the Métro and into the daylight. Close beside me, a man in a steel helmet was bellowing, 'Out! Out!'

'*Peut-être une bombe en cadeau,*' Chantal said with a smile. She pressed on amid the indignant Parisians. The streets grew emptier. Now she walked faster and looked up a lot.

FAILLARD was written on the venerable sign above our heads. Nine, eleven—we crossed the street—number twelve. My eyes leapt to the entry bell; Chantal's finger pressed it. I prayed to the god of concierges. Seconds crept by. A buzzing sound, and then the door opened a crack. Chantal thrust her hand inside. We slipped past the little booth before anyone could look out of it.

I climbed the stairs slowly, reading the doorplates in the dwindling light. Old French names. Where was Hirschbiegel's proxy's name?

Fourth floor, last chance. Would there be a lock the silver key would fit into? I was still on the top step when I read the gold nameplate: WASSERLOF. Relieved, I stepped to the door.

'What about your friend?' Chantal asked as I carefully pushed the key into the keyhole.

'He's not here.' I stuck the key in too deep, pulled it back a little, wiggled it, concentrated all my feeling in my fingertips. The key wouldn't turn. Chantal stood behind me, waiting. I licked the sweat off my upper lip. Changed hands. Leaned my forehead against the door. The teeth made contact, and there was some play in the lock, but nothing in it moved.

'Let me try.' Chantal gave me an energetic push to one side, wiped the oily key dry on my jacket, and effortlessly unlocked the door. It sprang

103

inward, as though it had been under tension for a long time. The bottom of the door squealed against the floor; the floorboards had warped. Chantal gave me back the key and let me enter first.

Semidarkness. Two rooms, the bedroom facing the street. Furniture the likes of which I'd never seen. Everything looked *installed*, somehow. Dark wood, trunks, hinges. At first sight, there were no German emblems, nothing that could remind Chantal of the enemy. Old newspapers, all in French. In the kitchen, Russian tea.

'Does your friend go to sea?' She was standing in the middle of the bedroom. The evening sun shone through her dress.

I realized that the room was outfitted like a ship's cabin. Everything made of teak and screwed down tight, as if the possibility of stormy seas in rue Faillard was not to be discounted. The furniture was nautical.

Steps from below. I stood still, but Chantal blithely went to the window. One floor down, a door was unlocked. The tenant left. Accordion music came from somewhere. The shutters were closed; Chantal opened one of them and let some air into the flat. I stepped behind her; she turned around. Inch by inch, with downcast eyes, she sank onto my chest. Her forehead lay against my shoulder. With great care, I wrapped my arms around her. Fabric brushed across fabric.

'What's that?' She pressed her fingers against my back.

I remembered my ID tags. Name and number, Wehrmacht corporal.

'Nothing,' I said, stiffening.

'That was something.' She tried to find the spot again.

'It's an amulet. A lucky charm.'

'Why do you wear it on your back?'

I disengaged myself from her. 'I'm all sweaty,' I said, and left the room. Out in the hall, I had two doors to choose from. I opened the broom closet, closed it, went into the bathroom and shot the bolt.

Soap, toothpaste, talcum—all German brands. I ran the water. Gathered the stuff together, opened the transom window, and threw everything into the air shaft. A tinkling sound came from far below. I couldn't get my belt off; my buttons seemed too small. I slipped my shirt off nervously, removed the chain with the tags, and hid them in the laundry hamper. Then I washed myself. A silk bathrobe hung on the door.

'Antoine!' she called from outside.

'Yes?'

'What's your real name?'

I pulled the robe on and tied the cord. 'My name is Antoine!' In the mirror, there was no longer anything German about me.

When I stepped out, Chantal was standing in the bedroom. She bent over the mattress, which was firm and tightly packed; it probably came from the Reich. As she straightened up, she smiled at the robe. It was too short for me.

'Now I have to know,' she said. 'Why did you do it?' I was silent. The cold silk gave me the shivers. 'Perhaps'—her eyes grew scornful—'because you're a Frenchman *at heart*?' She sat on the edge of the bed. 'Or is it just that you don't like the war?'

'War's nothing special,' I replied gruffly. 'There's always war.'

'Then all that's left is the French solution to the puzzle.' She seemed sad for a moment. 'You did it for a woman.'

I looked away, toward the window. Outside, things were turning blue. I thought about Leibold. Maybe, at this very moment, he was lying on a bed like this, but his mattress was French and he sank into the middle of it, staring at a blanket like ours. He'd had bad luck today, but at some point the image of the kissing couple would return to his mind, and maybe he'd realize who it was he'd been looking at. If he thought about it long enough, he might even come to a conclusion. How much time did I have left?

I sat beside her, looked down through the opening in my bathrobe, and contemplated the folds of my skin. We held hands. Hers were brown and sinewy. I couldn't begin enjoying this situation, this intoxicating moment, right away.

'Where are you?' Chantal grabbed me by the hair.

Her shoulders; the blue ceiling. The evening had become heavy. I tried to get up again and close the shutters. She wouldn't let me go.

*   *   *

I woke up suddenly during the night. Wanted to know why. Melodies came to me, but not sung, only thought. Chantal's leg lay across mine. Slowly, I stroked her thigh and her knee, contemplating her beautiful, relaxed body, her regular breathing. When she turned her head and her hair fell over

106

her face, I gently pushed it aside. The next moment, she bounded from deep sleep into glassy wakefulness.

'Are they coming?' She drew away from me and sat up.

I tried to pull her back. She pressed her shoulder blades against the headboard. 'What time is it?'

I gestured toward the window. Everything was still black outside; no grey shimmer yet.

'Chantal—'

'Yes?'

'I can't remember this song.'

'Song?' She shook her head in the dark.

'A popular tune.'

'And how should I—'

I scooted closer to her. 'If I don't remember it, I won't be able to go back to sleep.'

She slowly stroked my collarbone. 'You're the craziest *boche* they've ever sent here. So how does this song go?'

I hummed a few notes. 'It's about a girl. Someone loves her in April. In the summer, she's alone again.'

Chantal nodded. 'In April,' she repeated gravely.

I remembered some words: *'Avril prochain—je reviens.'* Deep, brief notes. 'Do you know it?'

Chantal sang in her boyish voice. The result was a new, unwieldy melody. I pulled the covers up and felt drowsiness returning. Chantal was wide-awake now. She began to caress me, refusing to let me fall asleep on her breast. She sniffed my armpits, my belly, and slid on top of me. The oval of her navel, a dark moon, danced up and down.

*   *   *

107

Chantal washed her underarms and her breasts. I sat on the lid of the toilet seat and smoked. The windows were open. It was so early, the city was still giving only isolated signs of life.

'Why do you work in Turachevsky's?' I asked.

The hand with the washcloth slowed down. 'Don't go there anymore.' She turned her back to me again.

'Because of the money?' I felt the question pushing her away from me.

She bound up her hair and pinned it together on the nape of her neck. Covering her chest with her arms, she turned around. 'I don't want you to see me there.'

'Like the other *boches*?'

'Right.'

I stood up. 'This is the only place where we can meet.'

She gazed at me with tired, lascivious eyes.

'Tonight?' I asked.

'Maybe tonight.'

I threw the cigarette into the toilet. 'What are you going to do now?'

'Look for Gustave. They didn't get him—I can feel it.'

I contemplated the two of us in the mirror. She smoothed my shirt and hugged me. A horn sounded outside, in front of the building. We both flinched.

Chantal left first. 'I'll get here a little before eight and wait for you downstairs,' she said.

We didn't kiss each other again. Confused, I stayed behind in the strange flat, amid the ship's furniture. By the light of the rising sun, I removed

108

the Wehrmacht emblem from my underpants. I locked up carefully, kissing the key like an ally. On the way down the stairs, I considered whether I'd have enough time to take Monsieur Antoine's laundry bag to the hotel before I went on duty.

15

I put the bag under the desk. An SS corporal looked up briefly, then bent back over his lists. My table was the smallest and the farthest from the window. No one had called for me yet. I took my seat, reached for the transcripts of yesterday's interrogations, and began translating them.

Half an hour later, Rieleck-Sostmann stepped out of Leibold's office. I was hoping for a sign or a look that might indicate the barometre reading in there. Rieleck-Sostmann walked past me. 'He's waiting,' she said to my back. When I turned around, she was already filing papers.

I gathered up notepad and pencils, knocked on the door, and entered. Leibold was on the telephone. I came to attention; he took his time. At last, he hung up.

'Feeling better today?' He fastened the topmost button of his uniform. 'Did you go swimming?'

I stiffened my spine. '*Swimming*, Captain?'

'A splendid day for a swim.' He placed himself in front of the window in such a way that I couldn't make out the expression on his face. 'It was bloody hot while we were making our raid yesterday afternoon.'

I held my breath.

'So what did you do on such a lovely summer afternoon?' He blinked in the sunlight.

'Nothing special. Met up with a comrade.'

Leibold turned to the door, gripped the handle, and waited.

I understood: He wanted to know the name. 'Hirschbiegel. A lieutenant on Colonel Schwandt's staff.'

'Panzer outfit?' The captain looked at me steadily.

'Yes, sir.' I named Hirschbiegel's unit.

'What do you have to do with panzer officers?' One boot heel rocked back and forth on the floor.

'The lieutenant and I are billeted in the same hotel.'

'I see.' He opened the inner door; in the interrogation room, the corporals were on their feet and ready for action. 'We didn't get them all yesterday,' Leibold said with a thin smile. 'All the same, I'm satisfied.'

I felt as though an iron clamp were closing around my throat. I lowered my eyes, ostensibly to turn to a clean page in my notepad.

'Be careful,' the captain said.

The floor of the room seemed to sink. I pressed a pencil with two fingers. It would snap soon; I could feel it. Finally, Leibold went into the room. I followed him and took my usual place.

They brought in the barber.

He'd been beaten—there was an open wound over his right eye. They set him down on the chair. Leibold had his particulars read aloud: Gustave Thiérisson, residing at 31 rue Jacob. Proprietor of a barbershop.

He hadn't looked at me yet.

110

'Have you had your shop for a long time?' Leibold began.

'Le salon, vous l'avez depuis longtemps?' I asked him softly.

Gustave straightened himself. His handcuffs clinked. It wasn't his appearance that shook me; it was the hopelessness in his eyes. He stared at me.

At last he said in a cracked voice, *'Propriété de famille.'*

'Family property,' I said.

'And do you have a licence to operate a printing press in your *family property*?'

I hesitated a moment too long. 'Say it!' Leibold snapped.

I pressed my knees together and interpreted. The barber was about to speak, but they didn't wait that long. And this time, the captain didn't let me leave.

They struck Gustave in the face. He didn't cry out; he groaned and waited for the next blow. They let his pain subside and then beat him some more, throwing him to the floor, kicking his soft parts. Leibold didn't interrupt and asked no questions. He let them take their time. Eventually, they hauled the barber back onto the chair and opened his trousers. One of them put on a glove. Gustave gazed at me in bewilderment. Blood dripped from his eyebrow. He watched the glove approach his genitals. The corporal seized them. Gustave screamed wildly and twisted around to escape the other's grasp. His shoulders were yanked back. The one with the glove let go only when Leibold gave the sign. Gustave's body shuddered and twitched. He continued to scream, but as though from far away. Gradually, the

111

screaming turned to whimpering. A rivulet ran down his trouser leg and dripped onto the floor beside his shoe.

'From now on, I want precise answers,' Leibold said. 'Say one word I don't like and we do it again.'

I translated. My armpits and back were damp with sweat.

Leibold continued: 'Are you the owner of that printing press?'

I asked the question in French and added, in the same breath, *'Dis-le vite!'*

Leibold scrutinized me but said nothing.

The lacerated face, the broken nose. Gustave admitted to owning the press.

'There's a woman who works in your shop,' said the captain. 'What's her name?'

I translated. Gustave raised his head a little. Our eyes met.

'What's her name?' Leibold repeated. The corporals got ready.

'Dis son nom!' I shouted at the barber with exaggerated ferocity.

'Chantal,' he replied, his voice barely audible.

'Chantal what?'

'Joffo.' He stopped. *'Elle n'en a rien à foutre.'*

'The woman had nothing to do with it,' I said.

Leibold's eyes went from me to the prisoner and back. 'That remains to be seen.' He carried on with the interrogation.

Shortly before noon, the barber lost consciousness. The corporals tried to waken him by throwing water on him. When that proved useless, Leibold had him returned to his cell. They dragged his unconscious body out of the room; his feet thumped against the floor.

Away from the others, I sat down in the courtyard and had a smoke. I saw Gustave, his open wounds. One more session like this and he'd tell all. I sucked frantically on my cigarette.

'You should get more sleep.' Anna Rieleck-Sostmann stepped out of the shadows.

'It's just the heat.' My smile was unsuccessful.

She sat down, thrusting her legs into the sunshine. 'If I can help you, I will.'

'You think I need help?'

'You know this barber, don't you?' She leaned her head back.

My frightened look said it all. 'What makes you think that?'

'Don't play games with me.' Rieleck-Sostmann shooed a fly away from her forehead.

'I got a haircut in his shop once.' This statement was supposed to sound casual. She laid her hand close beside mine. 'Have you said anything to Leibold?' My finger touched the back of her hand.

'Why should I?' She took a cigarette out of my packet. I gave her a light. 'You're perfectly capable of doing yourself in without any help from me.' She blinked as a spark flew too close to her eye.

'Please, Anna—'

'I'll have some time today, I think. Shall we say six o'clock?' She gave me a sidelong glance. 'Don't forget your bag under the desk.' As she spoke, she stood up and left.

For several minutes, I stared at the patch of sunlight as it reached my boot and then my calf. My leg got very hot inside the leather shaft. I didn't move until one of the corporals ordered me inside.

16

I washed myself, scrubbing my feet and knees with the rough washcloth, even using the coarse soap in my hair. I avoided looking in the mirror and poured ice-cold water over my head by way of a final rinse. A short while before, the door had shut behind Rieleck-Sostmann. I was making an effort to erase the past hour from my memory. The powerful thighs, the flushed throat. I sprang out of the bathroom and tore three pages off the calendar. Then I put on the good uniform, bought a bottle of cologne from the toilet attendant, and daubed it on my throat and temples.

There wasn't a star in sight, and hardly any civilians in the street. I walked out into the evening haze and encountered the usual mixture of officers and enlisted men sauntering about, looking for pleasure. Once, I thought I heard steps behind me, but the sidewalk was empty.

I went straight to rue Faillard, no detours. When I reached the building, a fearful feeling came over me. My hands were damp; I ran my fingers through my hair twice before I pressed the doorbell. Once again, the concierge remained a phantom behind a curtained door. Only a cough revealed that someone was in there.

I whispered Chantal's name loudly into the stairwell; no answer. I climbed up to the flat and waited in front of the door. She could have been delayed somewhere, I told myself. At the end of half an hour, I was certain she wasn't coming. It took me a long time to get the door open, but it scraped over the floor again at last. The flat seemed musty and unfamiliar today. Only the pillows and sheets were reminders of last night. I found a bottle of wine in the kitchen. Without turning on a light, I sat down on the ship's sofa and drank. Later, I poured myself some of Hirschbiegel's cognac and I drank it in big gulps.

When both bottles were empty, I opened the window and paced around the flat, oppressed by my own helplessness. I felt sick, spat up the burning liquor, and made a dash for the exit downstairs, stumbling on the smooth steps. My boot heels were intolerably loud. I ran past the concierge's booth, headed toward the river, and didn't slow down until I was walking on the stone pavement of the bridge. I saluted as I passed two SS sergeants and made my way through narrow side streets, avoiding the vicinity of rue Jacob.

A clock was striking ten when I reached the black gate that opened into rue de Gaspard. Darkness everywhere. I entered the narrow street. The junk dealer's shop was boarded up, as if he had left it forever. I reached the bookshop and sat down on the big rock to catch my breath. Sweat ran down over my eyebrows. Suddenly, something in the darkness made me leap to my feet. Was the shop under surveillance? Were they already waiting out there in the dark, ready to strike at any moment? How foolish to come here! Dangerous for Chantal, as well. I reached the top of the steps in one bound and knocked on the door. It opened with a squeal, making me jump. The shop bell failed to ring. Only then did I notice the broken glass. Even though I could see things only in outline, I could tell when I walked in that they'd done a thorough job. Cases had been tipped over; hundreds of books strewed the floor. By the flickering light of a match, I contemplated the devastation and then spun around suddenly, blowing out the flame. Had something moved in the street? I stood still and listened for several seconds. In the end, I cleared a passage for myself and reached the counter. The ledger lay in pieces at my feet. Files, pictures, and folders were scattered about. The storeroom in the rear of the shop was in the same condition. They'd thrown the whole stock of books into a heap on the floor. My efforts exhausted me; I sat down on the book mound and took off my forage cap. I cursed the circumstances that had thrown me together with these people. Whatever I did would put them in danger. I accused myself of having informed on Chantal. Hadn't I forced the barber to say her name? Would I be facing her tomorrow at her interrogation?

No sound of any kind except the rustling of paper. My cap slipped off my lap and fell to the floor. I groped for it and discovered one corner of a carpet that was covered with books. I straightened up. By the light of another match, I inspected the floor. Stamped on it; it was hollow. I pricked up my ears, but all was quiet in the shop. I found a candle and lighted it. Then I started raising the empty, overturned bookshelves and stacking the books against the walls. Slowly but surely, I cleared everything off the carpet, then stood at one corner, grabbed a handful of the dusty fabric, and pulled it back. With the toe of my boot, I looked for an edge or a dip in the floor. The air in the room was stuffy, so I took off my uniform jacket.

The notch in the floorboard was barely noticeable, even when I held the candle over it. Wax dripped onto my hand. The boards were smooth, except for one splintered spot, as though something had been attached there. Searching the room to see if there was anything I could use as a lever, I noticed a poker leaning on the wall behind the cast-iron stove. The handle was strangely thick, and the shaft tapered only slightly. I put the candle on the floor, jammed the flatter end of the bar into the floorboard, and put all my weight on the other end. There was a long, drawn-out creaking; it felt as if something was on the point of snapping. Suddenly, the trapdoor came free. A small crack opened. I remembered how I'd been dragged down there weeks before. I put my foot on the first step and cautiously began climbing down. Reaching the packed-earth floor, I held the candle high and turned in a circle. Rough brick walls; against one of them, a rack with potatoes and apples.

'I'm aiming right at your heart,' said a voice from the darkness.

I sprang back.

'Stay where you are!' he cried out.

'Joffo?' I blew out the candle. No answer. 'I'm alone.'

'Why should I believe you?'

I reached for the matches. The box slipped from my hand, and I felt around for it on the damp floor. Soon the candle was burning between the bookseller and me. His face was filled with anxiety.

'How long have you been down here?' I asked.

'They came so suddenly, I couldn't get away,'

Joffo replied.

'Does the cellar have another exit?'

'No.'

'How did you intend to get out?'

'I tried. The trapdoor was too heavy.'

'You might have suffocated.'

'No.' Joffo held the pistol in the light. 'Not while I had this.' He started climbing upstairs. 'They'll be back.'

I followed him. 'Where's Chantal?'

'Gone.'

'Where?'

We were standing side by side. He closed the trapdoor and pulled the carpet over it. 'You won't see my daughter again, monsieur.'

'I'm not to blame for what happened!'

Joffo put the poker back in its place. 'I'm going to have to abandon my books,' he said. 'You *are* to blame for that.'

He blew out the candle and led me past the counter. We felt our way to the door. Before I left him, I told him about the barber. I didn't mention the torture. Joffo stooped and picked up the door handle, which had been torn off. It made a cold sound.

'Don't try to find us, monsieur.' He looked back at his devastated world of books. Without saying good-bye, I slipped away, pausing a moment beside the rock on which I'd seen Chantal for the first time. I tried in vain to remember what she'd been reading then.

17

That night, I extirpated all Geman traces from my clothes, underwear included. Brand names were eliminated. Imprints were rendered unrecognizable. Even the numbers on the soles of my shoes—their German size—had to go; I dug them out with my knife.

The next day, I asked Leibold if I could discuss something with him. We weren't standing in our usual spot by the window overlooking the garden. This time, we were in his office. 'I'm a corporal in the Wehrmacht,' I said, 'and for that reason I request to be transferred back to my old unit.'

'Don't you like working in rue des Saussaies anymore?' Leibold's tone remained friendly, but I sensed he was lurking behind it.

In recent weeks, rumours of an Allied invasion had encouraged the French Resistance forces to intensify their efforts considerably. Every day, dozens of arrestees came through our department; the questioning of a prisoner was often a mere preliminary to his execution by firing squad. I admitted to Leibold that I was finding the interrogation sessions hard to take.

'These people are enemies of the Reich!' the captain replied, stressing each word. 'If you were at the front, you'd have to kill such enemies with your own hands.' In the silence, we could hear a truck drive past. 'Is that what you want, Corporal?'

The sun painted a hard-edged cross on the whitewashed wall. I stared at the patch of light behind the captain.

'I'm requesting a transfer,' I repeated. My voice sounded strange to me.

'You'll be informed of my decision.' He bent over his desk.

That same day, I translated the interrogation of two Frenchwomen who had broken *into* a prison camp in order to see their men. When I left the typing room late in the afternoon, Rieleck-Sostmann was conversing with an SS lieutenant. He told her that the barber they'd detained had died of his injuries.

*   *   *

'Greece, if you're lucky,' Hirschbiegel said. We were sitting side by side on his bed. 'Maybe Romania. Do your best to get to the mountains.' He was kneading his pink hands between his knees.

Outside, a lovely autumn afternoon was under way. The sky gleamed behind the rooftops of the buildings across the street. The air was cooler.

'Romania?' I tried to remember the map of the Balkans that my major had brought from there. Remarks were scribbled in pencil on the map: 'Partisan Corps 'Josip' ' or '12th Partisan Division'; it seemed that the war in the Balkans was being fought against bandits.

We fell silent; neither of us had mentioned Russia. Why should Leibold shrink from sending me there?

'Don't you want to see her again before you go?' Hirschbiegel asked.

'They're gone,' I said. 'They probably went to the country.'

'So rue Faillard goes unused.' The lieutenant sighed. 'What a shame.'

We drank cognac.

'Let me hear the song one more time,' I said. Hirschbiegel scooped some brilliantine from a jar and rubbed it between his hands. I stood up and went over to the shelves. 'Next April, I'll surely be somewhere other than Paris.'

When I found the brown record sleeve, he said, 'A mistake. I'm sorry.'

I pulled out the record. It was in two pieces.

'I sat on it.' Hirschbiegel's eyes were apologetic.

'Do you remember the melody?' I held the two halves together. 'How did it go?'

The lieutenant was rubbing pomade into his hair. 'It was just a pop song,' he said. 'What's the difference?'

I read the split title. 'Avril Prochain.' I couldn't remember the song anymore.

Shortly thereafter, we were strolling in the direction of the Seine, preceded by the scent of Hirschbiegel's violet water. The sky cooled off above the green-and-yellow plane trees, and it was growing dark very fast. I inhaled the soft air. The few clouds were brownish smudges. In the surrounding buildings, men dressed in sweaters lounged in the windows of the upper floors. A café was just opening; the garçon hadn't yet finished sweeping out. The sounds of various kinds of music came from all directions. We could hear fiddling in the distance, trumpet notes, a German song. An all-female group was playing in the restaurant across the street. We ambled over there.

Hirschbiegel fell for the petite violinist, a French girl right out of a picture book, who conducted the tricky entries with her bow. The violist was her opposite: robust and well-nourished. Her instrument rose and sank on her bosom with every breath she took. At the end of the waltz, the cellist gave me a sad look.

Hirschbiegel chewed a piece of French bread. 'Why don't you introduce us to the ladies?'

'All four of them?'

'The matron at the piano will be sent home,' he cried, laughing.

After a few glasses, he forgot the lady musicians.

'There's music playing *outside*!' The lieutenant stumbled out to the boulevard.

We pressed our way into the passing throng, which got denser with the approach of the blackout. The air was loud with voices and a thousand footsteps and the stamping of soldiers' feet. Moustaches thick as thumbs, gold teeth laughingly exposed. Blood-drained faces, despite the remnants of summer tans. Soldiers were standing in front of a pathetic display window, hands clasped behind their backs. They were pretty casual about the saluting regulations, and there were few officers out and about anyway. I noticed a small sergeant hurrying across the same intersection for the fourth time, acting important, like someone late for an appointment, even though he was nothing but lost and alone.

Women outnumbered soldiers. Hirschbiegel imagined that every female who showed so much as a bare calf was a professional. Every few metres, he'd whisper loudly, '*She's* one for sure!'

Wooden soles, costume jackets slung over shoulders. They crowded the street in groups of two or four, putting their heads close together and

122

laughing. I listened to the fragments of broken German the girls used to start conversations with the soldiers. *Paß mal uff—auf Wid-dersen.* Laughter, cheekiness, nothing extreme. The real professionals stood out like racehorses in a herd of clueless ponies: high heels, furs on their shoulders. Exhibiting, being ogled, haggling with their eyes, disappointedly moving on. We passed a dashingly dressed boy standing beside the entrance to a café and insisting to the waiter, *'Mais j'ai douze ans.'* We passed an old woman wrapped in a green wollen shawl and sitting as though petrified in the darkness of her newspaper stand.

I opted for a café on the quai de la Tournelle with a view of Notre-Dame.

'Now what?' Hirschbiegel looked around impatiently at the other customers.

'Now we wait until our lucky break comes along.'

He eyed the couples around us sullenly. To do nothing but sit there thwarted his desire for conquest. 'I've had enough stag evenings recently to last me a long time,' he grumbled.

I enjoyed the breeze coming off the river. A short while later, two young women appeared. Proper skirts, starched blouses, pretty little hats on their heads. After a brief exchange, they decided to have a seat in the café. Hirschbiegel's spine stiffened when they headed for the table next to ours. He wiped his glistening forehead with the back of his hand. 'I like the tall one with the full shirt,' he whispered. 'You mind taking the delicate one?'

I agreed without really looking.

'What can they be, do you think? Seamstresses? Schoolteachers? They're not commercial girls—

you can tell that right away. When are you going to talk to them?'

I let ten minutes pass before undertaking anything.

He pressured me. 'Before someone snatches them away from us,' he said.

And in fact, an elegant Frenchman appeared at the neighbouring table and started a conversation.

'Now the frog's beating us to it!' Hirschbiegel squirmed in his chair. 'And the big one was exactly my type.'

The women gave the Frenchman a friendly rebuff. He shrugged his shoulders and turned back to the friends he was sitting with.

Hirschbiegel poked me. 'Your turn, buddy!'

I leaned over to the next table. *'Excusez-moi, mesdemoiselles. On n'a pas encore dîné, mon copain et moi. Et nous ne sommes pas d'accord quel restaurant choisir.'*

'Mais il y en a des excellents dans le quartier,' the delicate one said.

'What? What's she saying?' Hirschbiegel was sitting in a pose, like an equestrian monument.

'Les demoiselles n'auraient pas une petite faim, par hasard?' I asked.

'Une toute petite faim toujours.' The big girl laughed.

'Look how she laughs,' the lieutenant said rapturously.

I explained to him that these two couldn't afford an expensive place.

'Tell them I'll pay for everything!' he declared. 'The best, nothing but the best!' Hirschbiegel was childishly happy, clapped for the garçon, and would not be dissuaded from paying for the ladies' drinks, as well. He suggested a posh restaurant.

By the time our meal was over, the curfew had long since begun. Hirschbiegel's luck made him patronizing and timid at once. He proposed that we all go to rue Faillard for 'a nightcap.' The big girl, a worker in a button factory, took his arm. The delicate one trotted beside me in silence.

We reached the narrow, darkened street and then the apartment building. I was working on an excuse I could use to get away without spoiling Hirschbiegel's adventure. I had no desire to go up to the flat. The lieutenant took his companion by the hand and pushed her finger against the doorbell. The abrupt buzz sounded in reply. Before Hirschbiegel pushed the door open, I noticed a movement in the shadows and flinched; ever since the afternoon in rue Jacob, the fear of being followed had taken root in my heart.

Footsteps approached. Chantal stood on the edge of the curb. She assessed the women and Hirschbiegel, looking for answers to her questions. Then she called softly, 'Antoine?'

I was so happy, I didn't know what to do. I ran to her and hesitated. 'You're still in the city?'

She was wearing a heavy jacket and carrying a bag in one hand. 'You're not alone?'

'Yes I am, yes I am,' I stammered. Then I turned in Hirschbiegel's direction.

The lieutenant walked over to us. 'Is that her?' he asked, bursting with curiosity.

'This is my friend,' I explained to Chantal. 'The one who owns the flat.'

'The *Jew*?' Despite the unreality of the situation, she smiled. 'Can I talk to you?' A glance at the women. 'It won't take long.'

125

'Where are you two going to go?' Hirshbiegel asked.

'Anywhere,' I said. She looked at me.

The large man inserted himself between us. 'Here,' he said. With a cordial nod, he handed me the silver key.

'What about you?' I kept hold of his hand.

'There are plenty of hotels.' He made an awkward bow and returned to the two French girls. In laborious fragments, he explained that the three of them would have to move on. Protests, laughter, and then their footsteps fading away.

'Why are you still in Paris?' I asked.

'I'm leaving tomorrow.'

Lost, dubious, and happy, I stood on the edge of the curb.

18

'Chantal, I love you,' I said hoarsely.

'No,' she whispered in the darkness.

'I won't be in Paris much longer.' I moved closer to her face.

'Why not?'

'I requested a transfer.'

'Good idea.' She touched my cheek. 'Anyone who speaks our language as well as you—'

'Where I'm going, French won't do me any good.'

She gave me a questioning look and put her arms around me. We kissed. She unhooked her dress and let it fall to the floor. We slid onto the bed. She captured my tongue between her teeth. I

126

stroked her long, suntanned thigh. Her pelvis moved slowly. Tenderly, she took me inside her. Her soft breasts. I swirled her thick hair and pushed all thoughts aside. This night outshone everything. It was borrowed time. Afterward, I poured us some wine and spoke about what the future would bring. About a *free* France.

Chantal laughed, her eyes half-closed. 'My father has a soft spot for the emperor.'

'Napoléon?' I touched her back.

'Papa's not a monarchist.' She looked at me. 'But before the war, he was against anything he thought sounded like a coup d'état.'

'And you?' I examined every one of her vertebrae.

'I still had short hair back then,' she said, smiling. 'In the evenings, after work, Papa and Bertrand often used to sit together in the storeroom. Bertrand is Gustave's father. In those days, *he* was the barber.'

'The white-haired man who reads the newspaper?'

She nodded. 'He was an ardent leftist, a member of the *front populaire*. He tried to convert Papa. Papa said, "The people demonstrating in front of the Bastille should go for a walk with their families instead. That's a better way to spend a Sunday."'

Sitting naked on the bed, I tried to imagine the times to come after the war, as if my mere thoughts had the power to create them. I forgot about devastated Europe and evoked an island of normality. I could tell from Chantal's averted gaze, from her meagre replies, that she didn't believe in such a future. For her, the present was too urgent and uncertain to afford a glimpse even of tomorrow. The war was going badly for the Germans now, yet she still saw nothing but foreign uniforms in her city. It would be better in the country, she said. There were very few occupying troops in the vicinity of her grandfather's farm.

'The countryside can't be subjugated,' she whispered into the room. 'The countryside's stronger than the tanks that roll through it.'

From downstairs in the street, a German song reached our ears like a stray dream. I took Chantal in my arms and told her that Gustave was dead. She lay still, completely rigid. After a while, I realized that she was crying.

Suddenly, I said, 'I could go underground.'

She laughed through her tears. 'You—a deserter?'

The fact that she didn't take me seriously, not even for a second, annoyed me.

'You're not French,' she said. 'You're just a Frenchman in your dreams.' She ran her fingers through my hair.

I pulled my head away and declared that I intended to abandon the idea of a university education. After periods of great destruction, simple things are needed, I said. Wood and stone. I planned to employ my skills as a manual worker. People with such abilities would be in demand in Paris, too.

'Where will you go, Chantal?' Our breathing coincided for a few gasps and then separated again.

'Away from Paris.'

The thought that we were lying next to each other for the last time paralyzed me. I stared over at the window. Sounds announced the arrival of morning. Had Chantal said a single word, I would have gone away with her, to wherever she wanted, that very night.

She pulled the covers over her feet. 'Whatever happens,' she whispered, 'don't ever go back to Turachevsky's.'

'If I hadn't gone there, we'd never have seen each other again.' I smiled.

'Promise me.'

'It's hardly likely I'll have another opportunity to go there.'

'Promise me anyway.'

I laid two fingers on her mouth and made the vow.

'The *Fables,* you remember?' She rolled over so that she could see me better. 'Everything's in the *Fables.*'

I nodded. My head was getting heavy.

'All roads are in the *Fables,*' Chantal said.

The image of the fox and the grapes crossed my mind. I opened my eyes once more and saw her smiling at me. Outside, the blackness was gradually turning grey.

19

December was severe. I climbed over mounds of cleared snow, entered the headquarters building in rue des Saussaies, and looked on empty-eyed as the PFC in the security passage checked my papers every day as if for the first time. Then I climbed the marble steps, went into the unit offices, sat at my place, and greeted Rieleck-Sostmann.

My colleagues talked—guardedly, in approximate terms—about the Eastern Front. Of late, the catchwords were *redistribution of forces* and *breathing space.* Things were bound to heat up soon in the west, too. On the eighteenth, Rommel had arrived in Fontainebleau to lead the defence of the Atlantic Wall. This development caused some concern in rue des Saussaies. I didn't participate in the conversations, and no one invited me to join in. The others knew I had my marching orders.

The ambiguity of my situation and my service here, which was becoming more senseless and brutal with each passing week, was just about over. The necessary papers had been issued. Leibold had only to write in a date. Montenegrin-Serbian border area, specific locality unknown, a new company, new comrades. The days passed.

I found myself inadvertently staring at a situation report in an open folder.: '1. Russian Offensive Against Army Group South Ukraine./ 2. Defection of Bulgaria./ 3. Order to Evacuate Greece and the Aegean./ 4. Progressive Withdrawal from Southeast Bastion; Transition to Definitive Defence of Fortified Sava-Theiss Line.' The word *Definitive* was underlined.

I looked at a map. My new assignment would be there, in mountain country. The front wiggled through the karst like a snake run mad. I waited. This delay in my departure was pure torment, but I didn't speak of that to Leibold. Christmastime came closer. I hoped I would leave Paris before the year was out.

Stories shortened the time for me. I lived in them. As soon as I went off duty, I picked up a book. I read novels, tales, whatever I could get my hands on. I browsed the booksellers' stalls every day, bought something, and devoured the words. Sometimes I went through two books in a single evening. The ones I liked the best had to do with glory and the performance of great tasks. At night, I thought about Chantal, imagining her life in the country, conjecturing about what she did during the brief, dark days, what clothes she wore, what she ate. I clung tightly to the belief that we hadn't said good-bye forever.

I seldom opened my door when Hirschbiegel knocked, which was generally late in the evening. His armoured infantry unit was being transferred to duty on the Atlantic Wall. He'd experienced war as a cakewalk for three and a half years, and now he was supposed to face the Allied invasion force, of all things. The lieutenant was happy because he'd been posted to the western portion of the Normandy coast and not to the Calais sector, where the attack was expected to come. His baths got longer and longer; he concealed his nervousness behind Bavarian grumbling. On the rare evenings when I went out with him, I felt uncomfortable and went back to the hotel early. I'd already said adieu to the city; Paris was the past.

So the invitation was all the more surprising. 'Christmas party,' Leibold said.

We were standing beside our preferred window, looking out at the garden. Snow was weighing down the unmown autumn grass. Leibold had recently started smoking continuously. His nicotine-yellowed fingers clashed with his well-groomed hands. 'We'll take the opportunity to

131

drink to your transfer.' He dropped ash from his cigarette and smiled.

'Has it gone through?' I asked the question as joyfully as if Leibold were granting me home leave.

He named the nightclub where the party was going to be. 'We're starting early. There's a colonel coming in from Chartres, and he has to go back there later tonight.'

I promised to be at the nightclub, which was near the Trinité stop, shortly before eight o'clock. 'Might I bring someone with me?' I asked. Leibold shrugged his shoulders; his hands clasped behind his back, he returned to his office.

Back at the hotel, I changed my clothes, climbed up to Hirschbiegel's room, and told him about the invitation.

'I'd rather not,' the fat man said, carefully checking around his bathtub to make sure everything was ready.

'We wouldn't stay long. They have to go back to Chartres tonight.'

'I have an aversion to the death's-head boys,' he answered. 'Besides, if my colonel found out I went to an SS Christmas party, there'd be hell to pay.' Hirschbiegel stepped out of his tent-size underpants.

I leaned my forehead against the windowpane. 'Leibold's not the worst,' I muttered.

While the lieutenant soaked his large body in hot water, I described the place and the women one could meet there. Gradually, he fell in with the idea. We left at 7:30. On the way, Hirschbiegel pointed at a poster for the collaborationist speaker Philippe Henriot. Over their compatriot's mouth and nose, the Resistance had pasted a notice: *A*

132

'Shouldn't you report such a thing?' he asked, smiling and nudging me. I stuck my hands in my pockets.

At Leibold's table, there were two decorated majors, a pair of adjutants, and a colonel who turned out to be from the First SS Panzer Division.

When we walked in, Hirschbiegel held me back. 'Why not bring Himmler along, too?' he said. Grumbling, he followed me to the SS table.

Leibold introduced me. 'When things get French, Corporal Roth is very handy,' he declared, anticipating the amazement of his fellow officers, who otherwise wouldn't have tolerated the presence of a corporal at their table. Leibold offered me the seat next to his. Hirschbiegel wound up sitting in the midst of the black uniforms. He was giving me evil looks, because there was nary a woman to be seen in the whole place.

The nightclub proved to be a total disaster. The brass from Chartres considered the wine an affront. The maître d'hôtel apologized; his *good* stock, he said, had been confiscated in a raid.

'It's your own fault for not hiding it better!' The colonel, an impressively large man with graying hair, laughed.

A change of venue was discussed. The gentlemen plumped for the usual nightspot itinerary, through the streets near the Seine. Then the conversation turned to its main topic, the rumoured invasion, but all in a tone that suggested the event would take place exclusively on a sand table. The Fourth Panzers moving west, supply lines secured, antiaircraft defences set up along

133

the Marne line. If Göring could just keep up production of the Junkers JU-52 bomber, the 'ol' JU.' Air superiority, that was still the key. In theory, the problem was solved.

Shortly before ten o'clock, the colonel said, 'There's this Frenchman who cooks for us. He recommended a club with a strange name— Polish, I think. Emil, do you remember what he called it?'

From the start, Major Emil had tried to converse with me in French, putting his vocabulary to the test. He was a rather formal but engaging fellow from Detmold. To my surprise, he knew the *Fables.* On the way to the car, he walked beside me and quoted from memory:

> *An ass who wore a lion's skin*
> *Did general fear awake.*
> *Though faint of heart, like all his kin,*
> *He made the other creatures quake.*

'So is there a Polish whorehouse hereabouts, or what?' interjected the colonel.

'Roth?' Leibold turned to me. 'Have you been back to Turachevsky's recently?'

Our destination was decided. Even though Chantal had been gone from Paris for some time, the idea of going to the very place where she used to work excited me.

Not much conversation in the automobile. I looked out into the night; alternatively, from time to time, I considered Emil's powerful-looking hands and pretended not to feel Leibold's eyes on me. When we got out, Hirschbiegel placed himself at my side. 'These guys are even worse than their reputation,' he whispered. 'Please stay close to me.'

Leibold rang the doorbell.

Many girls were lounging in the salon. Madame swept in, obtrusive and officious. Faced with such a wide range of choice, the gentlemen from Chartres suddenly turned diffident. By way of relaxing the tension, Leibold proposed a visit to the bar. Madame accompanied us there. We got a table close to the stage, remarkably enough, because as a rule, the front tables were occupied first. The dance troupe was performing the usual nonsense. Emil wanted to sit next to me, but this time Leibold was faster. Hirschbiegel sullenly squeezed in between the two adjutants.

The champagne was just the right temperature. The gentlemen from Chartres applauded the dancing girls. After they disappeared from the stage, the colonel from the First Panzers assumed the alpha-male role and began to tell jokes. He drained his glasses of champagne all in one gulp, as if it were whiskey. 'Who knows the one about the rainbow trout?'

Hirschbiegel had grown more and more morose. After the first punch line fell flat, he excused himself, shot me a look, and disappeared into the salon. The gentlemen made remarks about the heavyweight firepower of the Wehrmacht. While I was watching Hirschbiegel's exit, I noticed someone in the passageway. A woman with rust brown hair, her clothes out of place in Turachevsky's—dark trousers, a heavy grey jacket. And she was carrying a bag. The woman resembled Chantal. A second later, she disappeared.

'I'll have to tell that one to the old lady,' one of the adjutants crowed.

'Then she's got to hear *this* one, too!' The colonel was radiant.

I slowly got to my feet.

Leibold's eyes followed me. He asked softly, 'See someone you know?'

I murmured an apology that was submerged by laughter, took the shortest way out, and entered the salon. The woman with the jacket was nowhere to be seen. Almost all the girls were gone. Two soldiers complained that they had only half an hour left and hadn't had their turn yet. No trace of Chantal. I started thinking I was mistaken. All the same, I asked a Greek woman in a kimono; she didn't know anyone named Chantal. Then, in incomprehensible haste, she dashed up the stairs. Except for the Wehrmacht soldiers all around, the salon seemed unusually deserted. I went to the door and glanced up and down the frigid, narrow street. Indecisively, reluctantly, I went back into the bar.

Three of the five musicians were on their feet, picking up their instruments. The bandleader was playing a piano solo—Offenbach, a march from *La Vie parisienne*—joined only by the valiant percussionist, whose high-hat pedal squeaked. I watched the other musicians disappear through the side exit.

The gentlemen around Leibold were still laughing. Their booted legs were stretched out under the table; the officers whinnied and gasped for breath. Their insignia jumped up and down. The colonel incited them to new outbursts. 'This guy forgets to send his wife flowers for her birthday. . . .'

Leibold spotted me at the bar. His questioning look was an invitation to return to the table. I pretended to have ordered a drink. The march began again. The percussionist kept looking at the grey-haired pianist impatiently, but he played on, as if he wanted to replace the entire band with his ten fingers. The Algerian bartender put two glasses on the shelf and threw his cloth over his shoulder. Grabbing up an armful of empty bottles, he left the bar, heading for the salon.

My eyes hastily scanned the room. No employee of the house was visible. The pretty cigarette girl, the old Romanian woman who always came out of the washrooms and bobbed her head in time to the music—I couldn't find either of them. A chilly premonition came over me. Most of the people at the tables were Wehrmacht. The few French were profiteers, black marketeers, the *other* Parisians. One remark flashed through my brain. Hadn't the colonel said that Turachevsky's had been *recommended* to the SS officers? And what about the woman dressed like a man and carrying a bag?

The Offenbach performance came to an end in mid-measure. Voices that had just been railing against the music overlapped the silence. A brusque confusion of human sounds. The percussionist darted to the stage exit like a nimble animal. The bandleader calmly gathered up his scores and pushed the bench away from the piano.

I squeezed past the men sitting at the other tables.

'May I speak to you for a moment?' My hand rested on Leibold's shoulder. He looked up wonderingly. The others were howling with laughter; only the friendly Emil noticed me.

'*Asseyez-vous,*' he said with a smile.

'Captain, I . . .' A glance at the piano. The grey-haired maestro was hurrying away from it, not looking back. There was no more time. I pulled Leibold up. Suspicion in his eyes.

'What's going on?' he asked, slowly following me.

To get to the middle aisle, I had to step over the colonel's legs. He leaned to one side, unwilling to let his laughing audience out of his sight. 'And when he stood in front of her with the bouquet in his hand, she said . . .'

The lighted red arrow pointing to the toilets struck me as the obvious choice. It was only a few steps away. The bandleader was just disappearing behind the velvet curtain. A loud hubbub of conversation filled the room. Someone called out, 'What happened to the music?' The vigilant captain was right behind me. No one stood in our way.

Something ripped. I didn't hear the explosion. Pain in my ears. Before I went to the floor, I saw the red arrow in front of me burst like a sparkler. Something struck my eye. Brightness. The light came in the shape of a cloud; objects were inside it. A perfectly round tabletop, fragments of the chandelier, iron supports, parts of chairs. What I felt as silence was its opposite. Everything burst; the room shook. Suddenly, we were inside a tremendously radiant vacuum.

Leibold was thrown on top of me, astonishment in his eyes. There was no resistance in his soft body; he lay over me like a blanket. The flames blazed up, and now it gradually became possible to

138

grasp what had happened. Wetness on my temple. I coughed, twisted myself, grabbed the captain by the armpits, and rolled him off of me. From the front, he looked unharmed. But when I set him on the floor, I felt his torn uniform. Blood on his back. His bright, unbelieving face.

I cautiously got to my feet. My left eye was blurred, my cheekbone bloody. I had no handkerchief, so I wiped my face on my sleeve. The silence, immediately afterward. Only a little smoke. There was a big hole in the floor in the middle of the room; the bomb must have been hidden there. Despite the charring, I could make out the black of the SS uniforms, the red armbands. The adjutants from Chartres had been literally blown to pieces; one was missing half his head. Emil lay to one side, his legs jerking. I stumbled over to him. Plaster from the ceiling fell to the floor beside me. The flames began shooting up all around. I bent over Emil and his open mouth, which couldn't scream. His abdomen was ripped open from top to bottom. I had a distant memory of army training, of our sergeant's voice: 'First aid for belly wounds!' I pushed Emil's guts back into his abdominal cavity, yanked his belt over it, and pulled it three holes tighter. The dying man groaned. I straightened up and stood over him. The colonel's body lay nearby. He was bent backward, his arms over his head, as if reaching for something.

Blood ran down into my eyes. Through the veil, I could see half-naked women rushing down from the stage, followed by the tenor with two buckets of water. Some civilians were crawling on the floor; a girl in a kimono leaned over one of them, a man in a charred suit.

Leibold was conscious, his hands feeling around behind him. I saw that his whole back was burned, the fabric of his uniform seared into his skin. At this point, he appeared to feel hardly any pain. I leaned him sideways against the wall and then ran into the salon, where the general flight was under way. Soldiers and girls in a wild tumult. I looked for Hirschbiegel in vain, nor was Madame anywhere to be seen.

'Where's the telephone?' I shouted into the uproar. No one stopped moving. Women ran up and down the stairs. I caught hold of one. 'The telephone!'

She pointed to an edged curtain. I pushed it to one side, found a corridor leading to an office, and kicked open the lightweight door. The safe was open; papers were strewn on the floor. Fans, a lace coat, a stuffed poodle, all left behind. I smelled Madame's perfume, snatched the telephone to my ear.

I went back to Leibold to wait for the arrival of the rescue squad. He'd managed to stagger to his feet but had collapsed after a few metres. The devastated room lay in semidarkness, illuminated only by a few flames creeping up the wooden panelling. The bar was smoldering. The buckets had rolled down into the bomb crater. There was no trace of the musicians or any of the backstage people.

'Why . . .' The captain spoke in a whisper. I bent down to him. 'Why did you call me away?' His eyes were dark. Rust-coloured spots on his skull.

The moment was burned deep into the backs of my eyes: Chantal in man's clothing. In a second, I

140

understood everything. Old Joffo and the hidden cellar; Chantal, who performed here as Pallas Athena, goddess of war. Her words took on a new, deeper meaning. *Don't ever go back to Turachevsky's. Promise me.* I grasped it all so painfully, I had to turn away from Leibold.

'Why?' he asked for the third time. Although he was now in great pain, he didn't take his eyes off me. 'How did you know?'

I lied. 'Something didn't seem right,' I said.

Outside, car doors were slammed. Orders echoed from the salon. Immediately afterward, uniforms: medics. A graying army doctor, a captain wearing old-fashioned eyeglasses, stepped among the bodies, occasionally lifting an arm or turning a face. When he got to Emil, he squatted down, examined him, looked surprised, and waved to a couple of stretcher-bearers. Leibold couldn't be laid on his back; supported by two medics, he shuffled slowly toward the door. I followed the three of them. Before stepping out, I turned around for one last look. The piano was open, its lid blown off, its strings hanging out. The strings trembled at the steps of the men who were hurrying to and fro.

20

The doctor said I was lucky. Had the splinter gone in one millimetre farther to the right, he said, they couldn't have saved my eye. He bandaged it up; for a while, the world was going to look flat to me. Dawn was lightening the sky when they dropped me off at my hotel.

I fell into a dreamless sleep. Shortly before seven o'clock, footsteps came down the hall. A single knock, and they were in the room. Men in civilian clothes. I was to get dressed. Before I could reach full consciousness, they began going through my things. I asked to know why. Orders, they said. I was to keep quiet. While I pulled on my uniform, fear grew inside me. I'd foreseen this moment a hundred times—since the day when I first changed myself into Monsieur Antoine.

They took my French books and personal photographs from the shelf, along with a journal. Luckily for me, the last entry dated back many months. When they took the suit with the little checks out of the wardrobe, and then the shoes and the hat, I clenched my teeth. The suit proved nothing, but I felt my cover was blown. One of them spotted the place where I had ripped out the label. They said nothing, asked me no questions; they simply took note. I was to hurry up. Every movement I made seemed strange with one eye bandaged. While I grabbed whatever was indispensable, an astonishing wish crossed my mind: If I were only at the front, I'd be spared the worst.

Footsteps above my head. They were in Hirschbiegel's room, too. I cursed myself for having been so thoughtless as to draw the lieutenant into my double life. I heard him upstairs, ranting in Bavarian dialect. As they escorted me out of my room, the confrontation on the next floor became physical. Looking up the stairwell, I could see Hirschbiegel, half-dressed and invoking the protection of his colonel. Two men in civilian clothes pinned his arms behind his back, but the stout lieutenant was too strong for them and broke their grip. 'Buddy!' Hirschbiegel shouted in great distress. Like an ox that recognizes the butcher. Before I could answer, I was prodded forward.

They put me in an unmarked car and drove me to my workplace in rue des Saussaies. This time, there was no going in through the main entrance, the one I had used every day; instead, they pulled up in front of a solid gate. This was where the transports usually stopped, bringing detainees to be interrogated or picking them up afterward. I was led through corridors whose existence I was aware of but in which I had never set foot. Dim lightbulbs hung down over thresholds; carelessly whitewashed walls went past in a blur. I tried to spot name cards on the cell doors, but there weren't any. Only black holes, on the other side of which men were languishing.

The cell door slammed shut behind me. There was no further word of explanation. I leaned on the wall. I had a sickly feeling I remembered from my school days, when I was about to take a test I wouldn't pass. On the plank bed, there were two folded blankets; the straw mattress looked freshly filled. The washbasin was dirty, but the water tap worked. The slop bucket had been disinfected. The bottom of the window was level with my head. If I wanted to see the street, I'd have to grab the bars and pull myself up.

I took off my jacket and laid it on the mattress to use as a pillow. I was cold. What heat there was came from a grooved pipe that emerged from the ceiling and disappeared through the floor. I covered myself with the blankets. If I closed my good eye and looked at the lightbulb through my bandage, it was like staring at a hazy sun. My wound burned.

Three SS officers were dead, and there were many wounded. The people responsible had to be found; news of the incident was bound to penetrate to Berlin. I tried to regard my situation with the eyes of those who would look at me through the peephole, take me from my cell, interrogate me. What had I done? I'd worn a suit with little checks. Nobody would understand my motives. High treason: the thought entered my brain uninvited and would not be driven away.

Don't ever go back to Turachevsky's. While I lay on my hard bed and felt my wound with my fingers, I was almost pleased by the thought that I'd wound up in this fix because of Chantal. I admired her. Pallas Athena had taken off her clothes for the hated Germans in order to blow them up afterward. I sat up. Hadn't I foreseen this outcome? Wasn't it a given, ever since I took the checkered suit out of the wardrobe, that my adventure had to end here? There would have been only *one* way out: the front. Short work, whether here or there.

I stood up, did some deep knee bends to start my blood moving, and began to walk. Six and a half paces in one direction, six and a half back. The metal bedstead, the bucket, and the washbasin floated past me. It was now full daylight, so they'd turned off the ceiling lights. Would they come for me today? They needed results.

144

21

I jumped to the window bars and pulled myself up. The day was clear and cold. The snow had been pushed aside so that it formed a trench. In the gallery across the way, an SS soldier walked slowly back and forth. He spat a long arc of saliva into the snow and bent over the ramp to see where it would land. The walls enclosing the courtyard resembled barrack walls. The cells were too dark to see if anyone was looking out through the bars like me. I let myself sink back to the floor and resumed my walk.

It was two years since I'd arrived in Paris. Eight wearisome hours in a flatbed truck before we reached the city. At the final rest stop, my major had fairly beamed with joyful impatience and slapped the seams of his trousers with his gloved hands. 'Every word, Roth!' he cried. 'I want to understand every word!' I had hoped he might invite me to ride with him in his Kübelwagen, but the major merely bounced on his heels, turned around, and climbed back in.

Shortly after that, we reached the outskirts of the city. A bomber had made a direct hit on a railway line—the crater was geometrically perfect. Sappers stood on the tracks, smoking; one of them waved his pipe at us. The men in the rear of the flatbed truck called out what they saw to those of us who were under the tarpaulin. A private from Franconia was sitting across from me. His craning neck formed a pale rectangle. 'Stop with the buildings!' he shouted. 'How about the women?'

'No one's on the streets,' one of the lookouts said. 'Except for our troops.'

The Franconian punched the canvas above his head. 'Goddamned tarp! When we marched into Paris, they had lots of open vehicles.'

Later, someone shouted, 'There it is!' The truck slowed down and entered a long curve. Elegant windows; trees in full bloom. We'd reached the Arc de Triomphe. What I actually *saw* could have been any building in any city. Then the wheezing quartermaster appeared behind our truck. 'Roth!' he called into the darkness, narrowing his eyes. 'Is Corporal Roth in there?'

I pushed the Franconian's knees aside, squeezed my way through, and jumped off the truck, which continued to move. The light was a dazzling white, blinding. The quartermaster steadied me to keep me from tumbling over. His glasses glinted.

'I'm taking you with me to P Four, P Six, and HJ Seven,' he said, paging through his list. The breeze ruffled his carbon paper. 'You'll be staying in the same hotel as the major.'

I stood on the Champs-Elysées. The trees lining it were so far from the middle of the street that I couldn't tell whether they were plane trees or lindens. I actually couldn't spot a single civilian. The sun turned the street into a bright wedge. The quartermaster hastened back to his Kübelwagen, calling back over his shoulder, 'Hurry it up!' I clasped my hands behind my back, raised my head, and stepped out like a field marshal. Only for a few metres. Then the truck's horn sounded behind me.

*　　　*　　　*

Weariness in my legs. And dizziness inside my skull. I leaned my forehead against the wall and looked out for the sun, which was now directly behind the building. I realized I must have walked back and forth in my cell for three hours without stopping.

Months before, I'd eavesdropped on a prisoner who was talking about his 'daydreams.' Time seemed like an unreachable horizon; intoxication came through the whitewashed walls, he said. In the second year of his solitary confinement, he'd dreamed for as long as seven hours a day with his eyes open while pacing the equivalent of twenty kilometres in his cell. He developed blisters without feeling them.

I wondered how my brain and my nerves would react to what was coming. Hundreds of men had been interrogated in my presence, and I'd watched how they changed in the face of death. When hope was extinguished and the body helplessly exposed to pain, something incredible happened. A person became someone else.

They didn't come for me that afternoon, or that first night, either. The meal procession went past my cell twice. I was hungry, but I didn't present myself at the door. Instead, I stayed flat on my back and tried not to notice the smell of meat and onions.

The next morning—it was before breakfast was brought around—I heard three evenly spaced taps. I sprang to my feet. Three more taps. I darted around the cell, listening over the washbasin, listening to the heating pipe. The sounds were coming from behind the plank bed. There must have been a pipe running through the wall. I

147

looked around for an object I could use. I hadn't received any bowl or spoon, and it would take too long to pull off my boots. I opened my shirt and took off my ID tags, then gave the wall three evenly spaced taps.

An answer came at once. I hoped the other fellow would use the quadratic tapping alphabet—it was the only code I knew. The wall didn't have much resonance. I had to lean my head against it in order to hear clearly. As I did so, I kept my eye on the peephole in the door.

The other guy was obviously a practised hand; he tapped unhurriedly. I pictured the square box: five horizontal lines, each with five letters. He tapped four times—the fourth row, *p* through *t*—and then five: *t*. Then a pause, followed by three taps, then five. Third row, fifth letter: *o*. Two, four: *i*. I understood: *Toi?* Names had no meaning here, but at least I knew my fellow prisoner was French. I lowered the hand with the tags. I was still a soldier in the German Wehrmacht; exchanging messages in tapping code with a Frenchman couldn't help my situation. I took a deep breath. There was no *situation*. Very soon, they'd know everything.

I began. One and one: *A*. Three, then four: *n*. As I introduced myself as Monsieur Antoine, my 'handwriting' became more fluid.

The other's name was Henri. He asked: Since yesterday?

Affirmative. He asked if there was any Paris news. I hesitated. He could just as easily be a political prisoner as someone in jail for an ordinary crime. I kept my answer general. We 'talked' for half an hour. The tapping stopped

148

suddenly, in the middle of a sentence. Then, hastily: Now.

I pictured a cell door above or below me being unlocked and Henri brought out. In my mind, they took him to my former unit, where another translator sat in my place. The corporals and the water tub stood ready.

It was only now, from one moment to the next, that I felt sick. I retched and bent over the toilet bucket. I hadn't had anything to eat, so nothing came up but whitish phlegm. I sank to my knees and heard my gasps reverberating in the bucket's metal sides.

During one of our chats by the window, Leibold had explained to me that any physical pain is bearable if one knows beforehand what's coming. Many subjects, he said, behaved as though they were undergoing a surgical procedure. They screamed and panted and waited for the moment when it would be over. Afterward, they were the same as ever. Only with the *unknown* could you obtain results, because it offered no standard of measurement. Faced with the unknown, the offender had no way of assessing his own powers of resistance and couldn't foresee how he would react. Every subject was affected by this anxiety, the fear that in this situation he might say something that could never again be put right.

I lay down on the straw mattress. Leibold had figured out a way of surprising every prisoner so far. Men with trained minds, brutes with broad shoulders and giant paws—none of them had left the interrogation room 'the same as ever.' All of them had been caught in *their* special place. Sometimes it took days, but the captain was patient and found the right way. The soft-voiced Austrian with the sad eyes, the man who loved mountains and knew plants by their Latin names, was a master of the unknown. It occurred to me that he'd been seriously burned and wouldn't be healed anytime soon. I'd be brought before someone I wouldn't be able to assess. I couldn't predict any part of the process except the result.

I rolled to my feet and started pacing again. The certainty of what was in store for me made me feel strangely at ease; the melancholy of the last weeks abated. I washed my face, arms, and chest with cold water, rinsed out my mouth, and dried myself off with my shirt. As I got under way again, I recalled the *techniques* I'd been a witness to. I tried to imagine the physical sensations they produced. But I knew that mental practice alone would not suffice. I knelt down, lifted the iron bedstead a little, and laid one hand under it. With the other, I pushed down on the bed, slowly, as hard as I could. The dull metal of the bed leg cut into the back of my hand; something threatened to break. I pushed harder and counted the seconds. After two minutes, I relaxed the pressure and noticed that my heart beat faster *after* the torture than during it. A dark bruise spread across the back of my hand; a deep square imprint was clearly visible. The pain radiated all the way to my shoulder. I was satisfied with myself. Suddenly, I felt an eye at the peephole behind me. Standing up, I resumed my walk as if nothing had happened.

22

The third day. The meal procession passed for the fifth time; the food smelled good. I didn't go to the peephole. I knew they weren't simply overlooking me; their neglect was purposeful. I wasn't a heavy smoker, but during those hours I longed mightily to combat my hunger with tobacco. By afternoon, my desire for a cigarette was overpowering. I hammered my fists against the door. It took fifteen minutes of this before a guard opened the little window where the peephole was set.

'Yes?'

'I'd like to buy some cigarettes from the canteen.'

'Have you got money?'

'It was taken away from me when I was brought here.'

'Then you have to write out a request to change your money into coupons.'

'I don't have a pencil.'

'You can buy a pencil from the canteen.'

'Without any money?'

I suppressed my rage and stepped back from the door. The little window closed. I drank water from my hands; the bruise had turned black.

That afternoon, I had the shivers. The wound near my eye started twitching. I was afraid the eyeball might have been damaged. I touched the bandage, loosened it on the side, and felt the spot where the burning sensation was. Even though it wasn't close to bedtime, I wrapped myself in both blankets and lay there trembling for hours. With my healthy eye, I examined the opposite wall of my cell, focusing on every uneven spot and learning the wall by heart, like a map.

The lightbulb went out. The sound of the last footsteps faded away outside. Once again, the food cart hadn't stopped at my door. I stood up and started walking in the dark. The rectangular glimmer of the window, six and a half steps; the door, six and a half steps. After a while, I imagined I heard tapping, but when I threw myself on the bed and listened, the sound had stopped. I took off my ID tags and tapped. Four, five, pause. One, one, pause. One, two. Henri didn't answer. Lying down increased the pressure in my injured eye. I sat up, pushed the mattress against the wall, and leaned against it. I was cold. An image crossed my mind, the memory of an older detainee who had fainted during a procedure. They woke him up with cold water. Then they punched his teeth out, he collapsed, and they poured more water on him and kicked his head. He crawled over the floor tiles. It turned out later that they'd damaged his inner ear and he wasn't answering the questions because he couldn't hear them anymore. When they carried him out, the floor was awash.

Suddenly, I couldn't remember what I'd just been thinking. I was aching for a cigarette. I stayed awake until dawn. My back hurt from sitting in a curved position for so long; my eye was throbbing. The shivering came over me in irregular waves. As the sky grew brighter, I finally lost consciousness.

Minutes later, the sirens woke me up.

23

At roll call the next morning, I demanded to be taken to a doctor. Two SS privates did the honours. We moved through a long gallery. Noises from the cells, the sounds of French. I could hear singing behind one door.

We passed a room with three high chairs. Clipping machines hung from the wall on long cables. This was where heads were cropped. The door at the end of the hall bore a red cross. One soldier escorted me inside while the other waited for him.

The doctor wore a white coat over his uniform. He was the same thickset man who treated the interrogation victims. He was smoking. I inhaled greedily. Many metal basins filled with bloody cotton balls and bandages were scattered about. A French newspaper lay on top of various medical instruments—forceps and syringes, an old-fashioned stethoscope.

'He has pain in his eye,' the soldier said to the doctor.

'Let's have a look.' The doctor balanced his cigarette on the edge of the table and took off my bandage. He removed the final layer with a yank, tearing off the scab. The pain bent me double.

'I'm a prisoner awaiting trial,' I gasped, 'and I have the right to be treated correctly.'

Unimpressed, the doctor picked up his cigarette and took a drag; with his other hand, he examined my wound.

'Not so bad.'

I tried to keep still. 'Is the eyeball damaged?'

'Won't be able to tell that until after the swelling goes down,' he said. He straightened up and looked at me closely. There was a tear-shaped birthmark between his eyebrows. I closed my good eye and saw a bright veil; the other's face was no more than a silhouette. I smelled his nicotine breath.

'I'll examine it again in a few days.' He dipped a cotton ball in a brown solution and daubed it on my wound. I drew in my breath through my teeth and nearly toppled over. The physician's voice came from far away: 'Stop making such a fuss. You act as though I'm taking off one of your legs.'

All my illusions about being armed against pain collapsed. My helplessness frightened me.

While the doctor was putting on a new bandage, I asked him, 'Would you perhaps give me a cigarette?' He and the private briefly exchanged glances.

'Take the pack. It's almost empty.'

The bright veil over my wounded eye disappeared again.

I could scarcely wait to get back to my cell. At the door, I asked one of the privates for a light. Seconds later, I was sitting on my plank bed, leaning my head against the wall and smoking. I savoured the mild burning sensation of the tobacco and held the smoke in my lungs for a long time. The delightful dizziness persisted until midday. This time, the food cart stopped at my door: buckwheat soup and a large chunk of bread. I plied my spoon greedily. After the meal, I took another walk. My pain eased a little.

When they came for me, dusk was already

falling. The sullen, solemn expressions on the SS privates' faces let me guess what our destination was. The heavy doors opened; we went past the shearing room and the doctor's office and down long flights of stairs. Marble hadn't been used so lavishly here as in the front part of the building. For the first time, I stepped into the courtyard I used to look down into every day. We walked over ice-covered stone slabs, falling into step together from force of habit. I spotted the garden shed. Was that where the one-armed fellow kept his scything rig? We reentered the building through an iron door.

The narrow stairwell was windowless and led to a brightly lighted room. I was told to wait. The privates left the room by the same door we'd entered through. On the other side, there was a *second* door. That's it, I thought. Whoever goes through here has arrived at the heart of the rue des Saussaies.

It was at least an hour before they finally came. Two corporals; I knew them both. They took up positions on either side of me. I stood up and walked purposefully between them into the next room.

I'd never entered my workplace from that side before. The desks were placed in such a way that the person under interrogation was in the jaws of a pincer. Beyond them was the narrow connecting door that Leibold and I had walked through every day. A uniformed secretary sat in the seat that until a short while ago had been mine. He was smooth-skinned, no longer young, and he kept his eyes on his paper.

The second lieutenant looked up from the file

on his desk. I recognized him; he was the one with the bleating laugh. We'd drunk schnapps together at Turachevsky's.

'Is someone treating your wound?' he asked. Nothing in his behavior suggested that he remembered.

I nodded and sat on the only unoccupied chair. The sharp look he gave me brought me back to my feet.

'Then there's nothing to prevent you from answering a few questions.' Now he pointed me to the chair, and we sat down at the same time. The clerk reached for his pencil.

'How is Captain Leibold?' I asked, and instantly saw that I'd made a terrible mistake. I was suspected of high treason; the man across from me was a superior officer. My attempt to act like a member of the family had the opposite effect.

'Since when have you been providing information to the enemy?' the lieutenant asked, his voice unchanged. He opened the file. 'Tell us the names of your contacts and describe the operations they're planning.'

If a prisoner answered the three standard questions immediately and completely, he was spared the worst. The previous night, a sentence has crossed my mind: 'You can't confess a lie.' I didn't know where I'd read it. Under the bright lamp, before the two corporals and the waiting lieutenant, I replied, 'I have never divulged any internal information. I have no contacts, and therefore I know nothing of their operations.'

The second lieutenant nodded as if this were exactly the reply he'd been expecting. 'We've got witnesses who have seen you in civilian clothes.

Why do you pass yourself off as a Frenchman?'

Only Rieleck-Sostmann could have betrayed me. Was she sitting in the next room at this moment, listening for the first scream? Was she wearing the grey suit that modestly covered her knees? Had she decided on a different hairdo?

'Who says they've seen me?' I asked.

'Do you wear civilian clothes in public or not?'

I said nothing.

He stood up. 'Insubordination and fraternizing with the enemy!' He raised his fist, but it was a studied gesture. Soon he'd give his desk a good thump. One of the corporals moved slightly. The guy—was his name Franz?—was getting impatient. With the French offenders, the prelude rarely lasted so long.

'Who are your contacts?' The second lieutenant's fist came down heavily on the desk.

'I have no contacts. I'm a Wehrmacht corporal, and I have—'

I noticed the lieutenant's nod. Almost simultaneously, the first blow struck me. It was as though my temple had been split in half. I flew off my chair; for several moments, everything was white. When I slowly looked up, the second lieutenant had a piece of paper in his hand. 'We know the perpetrators' names,' he said. 'Gérard Joffo, Chantal Joffo, Théodore Benoît, Gustave Thiérisson. Were you in contact with these criminals?'

'I . . . know two of them,' I replied with effort.

'You were in contact with them!' the second lieutenant cried.

'Gustave Thiérisson is a barber. I had my hair cut in his shop.'

157

The second lieutenant stepped closer. His booted legs towered over me. 'Would you have us believe you take off the uniform of the Reich, dress as a Frenchman, and associate with the leaders of a criminal organization *without* divulging any of the secret information to which your privileged position gives you access?'

'Yes, that's what I'm saying.'

At this point, I figured the corporals would start in on me again. Instead, the lieutenant asked, 'Where are these people now?' and walked back to his desk.

With a flash of hope, I realized that they hadn't caught Chantal and her father. As long as the lieutenant could assume I knew their whereabouts, he and his man would spare me. 'I don't know *exactly*,' I said, being careful.

'What does that mean?'

'I don't think they're in Paris anymore.'

'Then where are they?'

'I don't know the exact place.'

The second lieutenant waited until the clerk finished writing.

'Since when did you know about the attack in this nightclub, this Turachevsky's?' He pronounced the name awkwardly, as if the brothel were completely unknown to him.

I'd thought about this. If they knew about my 'double life' from Rieleck-Sostmann, they must believe I had something to do with the bomb. A grotesque story: German soldier falls under the spell of a beautiful Resistance fighter and allows himself to be enticed into colluding in the assassination of his own people. The actual facts were a bit soberer. I had *known* that Chantal was a

158

member of the Resistance. I should have reported her. Instead of doing that, I'd warned her people about the imminent raid. According to the occupation law, I was guilty.

'Do you think I would have gone to Turachevsky's if I had known about the attack?' I replied. 'Besides, I was wounded in the explosion, too.'

The second lieutenant's face turned stony. 'Three senior SS officers were killed, along with seven civilians. Two officers are in critical condition in the hospital, with life-threatening mutilations! Corporal Roth, however, survives with a scratch on his eye! What extraordinary luck the fellow has!' He leaned over the desk. 'You knew about the attack! You helped plan it and carry it out! Admit it!'

The SS corporals moved closer.

'I warned Captain Leibold in time for him to—'

I had put my foot in it. How could I have warned Leibold about something I'd supposedly known nothing about? I sensed that the men behind me would begin at any moment. At the same time, I understood that I *couldn't* tell the lieutenant anything, even if I wanted to. I knew nothing of Chantal's whereabouts or the location of her group. It became chillingly clear that there was no way I could avert what was coming to me. Images from the procedures flooded my mind. The water torture, during the course of which some people literally drowned. The broken limbs. The sleep deprivation, which turned even powerful men, men with all their wits about them, into stammering, self-soiling wrecks who entered a state of interminably prolonged semiconsciousness in

159

which they would reveal everything so that they might finally be allowed to sleep.

I was drained and desolated by fear. As they grabbed me and pulled me up, I tried to control my nausea. All the same, I retched, vomiting on a corporal's stomach. He cursed. The first blows landed on me at the same moment.

24

I awoke in a condition whose sole characteristic was fear of further beatings. The notion that torture victims grow accustomed to unvarying methods turned out to be hogwash; pain wasn't trainable. Every turn on my plank bed caused suffering the likes of which had been unimaginable to me until now. I tried to avoid the slightest movement, but lying still was equally painful. I located the places where the throbbing radiated from and palpated clusters of large lumps. I could scarcely find my nose; my injured eye was swollen shut. If I tried to open my mouth, pain shot through my face. My jaw must be broken, I thought. I had seen detainees dragged out of the interrogation room in this condition: The lower part of their faces hung bizarrely to one side; their jawbones and lips no longer obeyed them. I tried to picture my face and fell into a feverish sleep.

Fresh pains awakened me; the doctor was in my cell. I couldn't see what he did. He reset; he bandaged. I screamed, but it wasn't my voice. He murmured something about pulling myself together, then finished his work and left the room.

Later, much later, I found porridge and water next to my bed. I drank some water; it ran out of the corners of my mouth and dripped onto the floor. I didn't touch the porridge. When steps approached, I pricked up my ears in dread; when they passed by, I sank back down, relieved. Between periods of unconsciousness, I heard a distant tapping. Did Henri want to talk to me? I didn't have the strength to answer and couldn't concentrate enough to understand the alphabet.

For two days, maybe longer, they left me in peace. Although I never touched the porridge, I didn't feel hungry. One night, I threw up the water I'd drunk. I waited for Henri's tapping. I shoved my jacket under my shoulder so that my head was lying against the wall and listened for many hours, tangled in the images my thoughts evoked.

My stern mother came to me; she seemed older than she was in reality. My brother described how he'd been put on the fast track to complete his medical studies; there was an urgent need for physicians. He was accompanied by all the teachers he and I had shared, all wearing beards. One of them showed the company the golden clasp that had been bestowed upon him by His Majesty.

'My father has a soft spot for the emperor,' Chantal said.

She was sitting on the bucket in the corner, wearing the dress I loved most of all. The red dots covered her naked legs to the knees. She pulled the fabric taut between her thighs. How narrow her waist was. The dress was cut low and tight across her breasts.

'Which emperor?' I tried to sit up.

'Napoléon.' She reached the bed in two swinging

strides and sat down on the cool spot next to my knees.

'Papa's not a monarchist. He's just fond of ceremony.' She leaned over my hip and rested her elbow on it. 'Before the war, he was against anything he thought sounded like a coup d'état. He cursed the *front populaire*—he said their ideas would drive Germany to ruin.' Cautiously, I laid my hand on Chantal's thigh. 'I still had short hair back then,' she said, smiling. 'Papa and Bertrand often used to sit together in the storeroom.'

'The white-haired man who reads the newspaper?'

She nodded. 'While they were in the back, Gustave and I would be out in the shop, reading. Sometimes my father came in, ostensibly to make sure we weren't getting up to any funny business with the books. What he was actually doing was taking out another bottle of red. Bertrand was an ardent leftist, a member of the *front populaire*. He had a hiding place under the hair-washing basin where he kept a revolver, a small-calibre pistol, and a Mauser. He told Papa, "When the time comes for us to go out into the streets, I won't be late."'

My fingers registered the warmth emanating from Chantal, the barely perceptible movements of her thigh as she spoke. I would have liked to put my hand between her legs.

'Papa said, "The people demonstrating in front of the Bastille should go for a walk with their families instead. That's a better way to spend a Sunday."' She laughed out loud at the memory. 'Once I eavesdropped on an argument between Bertrand and my father. Papa got so furious, he

162

imagined himself at the head of a machine-gun detachment, rounding up the ringleaders of the revolution. He unmasked them as foreigners and Jews. Bertrand was highly insulted at being lumped together with Jews and left our shop.'

One tap. A pause, then three. Two more, then three more. Pause. While I was still thinking about the letters *c* and *h,* Chantal stood up. Henri continued. I lost the thread. I heard an *l,* maybe a *p,* but I couldn't find the connection. I hoped he'd start over when he saw I wasn't answering. Chantal had disappeared into the corner between the window and the heating pipe. With an effort, I rolled over onto my side, took off my ID tags, and tried to tap out the word *slowly.* Was I using the code correctly? Henri started tapping in great haste; it seemed to be of the utmost importance. As much as I tried, and as hard as I pressed my ear against the wall, I couldn't understand him. Eventually, I gave up and sank back down, and the tapping faded away. I fell asleep; I woke up. The corner by the window lay in complete darkness.

*   *   *

The next morning, my cell door opened differently from the way it usually did. The guard didn't come shuffling in to put porridge and water next to my bed. From the corridor, I heard the sound of heels clicking together. The stillness of men standing at attention.

Pulled and thin, as though reflected in a distorting mirror, Captain Leibold entered my cell. It took me several seconds to realize that he wasn't part of a dream. Although his back was bandaged,

163

he was wearing the black uniform. His jacket was draped across his shoulders; his cap concealed his head wounds. As I scrutinized him in those seconds, a transformation came over me. Leibold's come to my rescue, I thought. Only Leibold can help me. He's here to release me from my fate. The door closed behind him.

He stood there, pressing his lips together. 'You could have gotten away unhurt,' he said softly. Then he came a step closer and hesitated. His expression was sorrowful. I thought about what I must look like. The young man with whom Leibold had so liked to stand beside the window—his own people had smashed my face. I tried to say something but succeeded only in breathing loudly.

'Why did you stay?' He bent over me. 'You could have been gone long before the bomb went off.'

'I—didn't—know—about—it,' I murmured, and gazed at him, unsure whether he'd understood me.

'One second sooner, and it would have blown you to pieces, too.' He shook his head pensively. 'The people upstairs are agreed that you're a traitor. Do you know that?'

Nodding caused me pain. 'I'm not a traitor,' I managed to say. New pain in my lumpy nose; something wet on my cheeks.

'I don't know why you're keeping it up,' he said. 'You know the procedure.'

I swallowed and remained silent.

'It won't do you any good. Tell us what we *must* know. After that, things will go better for you. I give you my word.' I'd never seen his eyes so full of warmth.

'But you're going to shoot me in any case,' I whispered.

164

'Yes.' He smiled. 'We're going to shoot you. But it's over quickly.'

'Why didn't you send me to the front?'

'No one decides what's going to happen to him.' As though inadvertently, Leibold reached around behind him, where his bandages were. 'You're more important here. We have to know where this woman and her father are,' he added wearily.

'When will you shoot me?' I trembled, propped up on my elbows.

'When you don't expect it.' He observed me sadly. 'Don't rejoice too soon.' He went to the door and rapped on it. 'By the way, it's the night before Christmas,' he said. 'We're having a social evening. Comrades getting together. Too bad you won't be with us.'

The guard stood at attention as Leibold walked past him. The hollow sound of the door closing. I tried to imagine how they were celebrating Christmas Eve outside.

25

The next day, I was taken back to the doctor. He examined my broken jawbone reluctantly. My jaw was forced open, and he installed a bit of wire to hold the break together. The doctor, who was a rather elderly fellow, tinkered around in my mouth with the indifference of a mechanic. The only part of his face that moved was his goatee, up and down, as he chewed on the stub of his extinguished cigarette. The SS privates held me fast. I figured that Leibold had arranged this operation. He was a man who appreciated proportions; perhaps my disfigured face had disturbed him. After the doctor was finished, he counted out ten pills into a little metal box. 'For pain,' he growled resentfully, as if he couldn't see why pain was something I should be spared.

When I stood up from the doctor's chair, my knees gave way. The soldiers hauled me out and led me to the head-cropping room two doors down. The French barber was even grumpier than the doctor. His impressive beard grew down from his chin and neck to where it encountered the hair rising up from his chest. I was ungently placed in the chair; the barber took hold of the monstrous machine, the cable swaying up and down before my eyes. The motor stuttered and rattled as it ran. The bearded barber started on my temples and worked up. My small head wounds, which had just begun to heal, split open. The Frenchman simply sawed right over them. I jerked and twisted away; one of the privates pushed my shoulders down again.

'He's putting on a show,' he said to his comrade.

Clumps of hair flew to the floor right and left. I looked for a mirror. A mixture of curiosity and dread made me want to see the extent of the devastation. The only thing I saw on the wall was a single Christmas-tree branch with an ornament attached. When the rough work was done, the soldiers went out to the hall for a smoke. The barber inserted a finer blade into his clipper and started cleaning up the hair on the sides and back of my neck. He pulled my collar to one side with his free hand. Just as he did so, I felt his fingers shove a crinkling object into my shirt. It slid down

166

my back and stopped, hanging between my shoulder blades. In a flash, my pain was forgotten and all my attention directed to the *thing* on my back. Since the barber was behind me, I couldn't see his face, nor did I try to turn around. Soon he finished his work. While I was being led out, he cleaned the blades of his clipper. Not once did our eyes meet.

Back in my cell, I waited ten minutes. Then I opened my jacket and my shirt and felt around my back; the object fell to the floor. It was a tightly rolled piece of paper. I unfolded it with flying fingers. Only three lines:

> We know where you are.
> Answer Henri.
> He can do something for you.

The signature consisted of two letters: C.J.

I sank down onto the bed. The strip of paper lay in my lap. I read the words again and again. After several minutes of amazement, I raised my head and looked over to the corner next to the window, where Chantal had recently disappeared. I hadn't the slightest doubt that the initials C.J. stood for Chantal Joffo. At that moment, the wall of morose passivity I'd been erecting around myself for days collapsed. I sat on the straw mattress and cried. The wire in my jaw hurt; I opened my mouth and bawled.

Even though I was dying to get into contact with Henri, I let hours plod by. I thought up questions I'd ask later, phrasing them as precisely as possible. Finally, I set up my plank-bed telegraph office. Since I had neither pencil nor paper, I pulled a rusty nail out of the wall in case I had to scratch something down. I tested the heel of my boot as a tapping instrument, didn't like it, and rejected the drinking cup and the tin bowl, as well. In the end, I pulled out my ID tags again; they were small and hard-edged.

I began. Two, three. One, five. Three, four. At first, I went very slowly, but gradually I picked up speed. The letters automatically converted themselves into taps; I didn't count anymore and rapped out entire words without stopping.

Not a sound in reply. Maybe Henri was out of his cell; many prisoners worked in the canteen or with the cleanup crew. Possibly he was asleep. For the first time, I tried to picture him. Small and muscular, with coarse trousers and a shirt that was white when he was arrested. In my mind's eye, he wore a beret and smoked nasty French cigarettes. I smiled: I'd come up with a Frenchman straight out of a picture book.

Meanwhile, I kept on tapping. I tried the whole afternoon, getting up every now and then to look through the peephole. No answer from Henri. Had Chantal's note come too late? Had he been transferred or killed? Shortly before the food cart came, I gave up, hung my ID tags around my neck, and lay flat on the bed. I thought I'd give it another try later that night, even though it would be more dangerous then, because tapping in a silent cell block could be overheard more easily.

Usually, the arrival of the food cart was the most absorbing event of my day. But when the server stopped at my cell this time, I took the proffered bowl without even looking at it. I sat down and spooned the pap and felt the warmth in my

168

stomach, but my thoughts were elsewhere. Wasn't it absurd to hope for help from a prisoner? As soon as Leibold was sure I *didn't* know where Chantal was, I could consider my execution a likely prospect at any time. And yet, I had the feeling everything that was happening to me made sense. I escaped into a thick tangle of speculations and desires. In a state between sleeping and waking, I imagined a dramatic rescue from rue des Saussaies. French Resistance fighters, freeing a German soldier! In an old building like this, there had to be secret passages and hidden cellars unknown to the SS. Maze of subterranean corridors, escape in night and fog, getaway from Paris, reunion with Chantal. We'd be in the country when we met again, surrounded by trees in bloom, white smoke rising from the chimney, horses grazing in the paddock.

I put the empty bowl aside, sank back against the wall, and smiled. Sudden jaw pain reminded me that the wire in my mouth made smiling inadvisable.

*   *   *

I was shaken awake roughly in what must have been the middle of the night. No light in the cell except for the flashlight beam in my face. Hands pulled me up. No chance to step into my boots. I got dragged out in my stocking feet, pushed along all the corridors, down the stairs, into the icy courtyard. Pebbles cut the soles of my feet; I was shoved forward. I cast a brief glance up at the window where Leibold and I had often stood. He'll help me, I thought; Leibold's the only one who can.

The SS corporals, the clerk, everything was as usual. I was still only half-conscious—I hadn't slept so deeply in a long time. I staggered toward the chair. A blow to the chest made it clear that I was not going to be allowed to sit. Leibold entered the interrogation room through the connecting door. I breathed a sigh of relief. He wore his uniform jacket over his bandages. He took his seat, holding himself exaggeratedly erect.

'Chantal Joffo is in the vicinity of Metz, isn't she?' Leibold spoke calmly; his voice sounded absent.

'Metz?' Chantal had never said anything about Metz to me.

'Is Chantal Joffo in the vicinity of Metz?' he repeated.

Had they come down on Henri? Had my tapping betrayed him? 'I don't know,' I said in a daze.

Leibold repeated the question several times. I considered whether he was trying to give me some information. His eyes revealed nothing.

'I don't know anything about Metz,' I said.

He nodded as though that was what he'd figured. The corporals didn't intervene. At last, Leibold picked up the telephone and began a conversation. As he spoke, he gestured to the corporals to take me out of the interrogation room. We got as far as the small, bare holding room next door. I tried to sit down and was ordered to stand at attention with my face to the wall. The other two stayed in the little room. They sat, one on either side of me, and smoked. I stood there with my hands on my trouser seams. Minutes passed; I waited. Perhaps an hour went by before I finally understood. The

170

interrogation would not be continued. Standing there *was* the state of affairs. Until further notice.

I knew from a conversation with Leibold that they'd discovered this method by chance. An SS lieutenant had ordered a rather elderly suspect to be brought in for questioning, but shortly after giving the order, the lieutenant forgot all about it. Since the guards' orders were to escort the man to the lieutenant's office and nothing else, they left him standing there in front of the desk. Meanwhile, the lieutenant had gone home. The prisoner stood there for the rest of the afternoon and throughout the night, but at some point the following morning, he fell down in a dead faint. Although this had all happened through simple negligence, it gave them an effective, practical idea. After days without sleep, people under questioning got confused and gave away information no amount of beating could pry loose. In the harsh light of the interrogation room, they would nod off, their chins on their chests; blows and buckets of water awakened them. In the end, they broke down and confessed—so they could sleep.

I stood in the bright room. The corporals guarding me were relieved at irregular intervals. I was under observation every second. The situation became a torment sooner than I'd assumed it would. Military training had familiarized me with standing still for long periods of time, but on the drill field, you could foresee the end of your ordeal. Here, the endlessness of the procedure was what made it so insidious. I considered letting myself drop and faking a faint, but my dread of the blows that would bring me back to consciousness was worse than remaining upright. I tried different methods of shortening the time. One way was to count to a hundred with all my weight on my right leg, shift to the left, and count to a hundred again. As I repeated this process for the tenth time, I noticed that the circulation in my legs was slowing down and realized that it would be better to stand with my weight evenly distributed.

I kept on counting, for no particular reason. My back and shoulders began to ache. I tried bracing my hands against my hips. A shout from one of the corporals, and my thumbs were lined up with my trouser seams again. My head seemed brightly lighted inside, and then darker and darker. Later, I thought I saw a bit of red. The wall dissolved before my eyes until it suddenly became impossibly clear. I started projecting a mental map onto the flaking plaster. I invented landmasses and straits and mountain ranges, which I provided with colours. I couldn't maintain my concentration for longer than a few minutes. My body stopped going along and made its presence felt with full force. I nodded off and then jerked my head up; it sank down again. Someone cried out. I stood there with my eyes wide open and felt my chin trembling. The wire in my jaw. The wall went fuzzy; I believed I was still staring at it, but in fact I was already dreaming. My eyelids closed. I fell forward.

Two arms pulled me up; fists worked over my kidneys, my ribs. I gasped and they let me go. I got to my feet unaided. I thought at first that the blows had woken me, but this condition didn't last long. I tottered, pulled myself together, stood stiffly.

The procedure was repeated several times, escorting me deeper and deeper into a desperate state I was hardly conscious of. My eyes shut instinctively, but the remnants of my will forced me to stay awake. I shivered and broke into a sweat. My clothes seemed to have become too tight and were on the point of bursting. I had the impression that my feet were swelling up, that my entire body weight was flowing into my feet, which couldn't support me any longer. The light above my head began moving in a circle. The room expanded and then shrank until it pressed down on my shoulders. The blows striking me showed that I'd fallen asleep again. The next time I raised my head, Chantal stood beside me.

'Gustave was with the first troops called up to the Maginot Line,' she said.

'Chantal,' I whispered.

'Shut your trap,' the corporal cried.

I signalled to her with my eyes that I was no longer allowed to speak.

'Gustave wrote to me and said the older soldiers had imagined this war would be worse than the previous one—and now they found themselves worn down by monotony. The Germans didn't attack for months.'

Chantal raised one foot and braced her heel against the wall. Her skirt slipped up over her knee. I envied her because she was allowed to lean.

'To relieve the boredom, dancing girls performed for the troops, and so did actors. Once they even had Maurice Chevalier.'

This went right through me. I raised my head so carefully that the corporals didn't notice. 'Chevalier?' I asked, moving only my lips.

Chantal nodded. 'He sang for them. Do you

know how long the Germans waited to attack?'

'Until April,' I whispered. 'The offensive was ordered for April.' The wire hurt me when I laughed.

'This guy still thinks the whole thing's funny!' a corporal cried.

I heard them stand up, and I stiffened my shoulders.

'Maurice Chevalier.' I giggled.

The door opened; the replacements came in. During the few seconds afforded by the switch, I turned to Chantal. 'You know the song, the one about the girl in April?' I asked.

A kick in the back of my knee. I collapsed under their blows. When I raised my head, the window behind the men was full of light. I moved my tongue inside my mouth, groaning. It seemed to me I said something. They dragged me into the next room. Leibold was sitting behind the desk, stirring a cup of coffee.

26

I was awakened. Had I slept? I lay on the plank bed like a man coming out of a drunken stupor; my head was a dismal insect. How long had I been here? Was it the same day, or the day after that? How was it that they had let me sleep? I must have made some confession. A question tormented me: Had I known something I couldn't even remember? Why had they allowed me to go to sleep?

I sat up, not without difficulty. The sun was

174

behind the building, which meant it must be past noon. I made an effort to think clearly. If I'd revealed some crucial information, I was now useless to them, and soon they'd have me shot. If they hoped for more revelations, their decision to let me sleep was inexplicable. I didn't have much time left. I remembered the strip of paper—and Henri. I took off my ID tags and started tapping. Three, pause, three again. After a short while, an answer came. Henri was listening.

Confession? I signalled. Haven't a clue. Chantal?

Could he figure out my situation from those questions? Did Henri know Chantal personally, or had he been informed by another cell? In my imagination, I suddenly stopped seeing him as a picture-book Frenchman. Now Henri was a clever young lad who had contacts everywhere, dressed well, and pursued only his own interest. But this image also faded, and while I waited for him to answer, Henri changed again. I saw him sitting next to the heating pipe; he was wearing a black uniform and transcribing my taps. Frightened, I pulled back from the wall, but then I calmed myself with the thought that I wasn't important enough to justify such an expense of energy as phony tap messages and notes passed through the prison barber; that was too complicated for the SS. They could use their usual methods to find out whatever they wanted.

The sound of rapid tapping came through the wall: Tomorrow. Interrogation. Evening. Garden shed. Then nothing more.

Thoughts flooded my brain. Chantal belonged to the Resistance. Recently, its organization had become more refined. There were French civilian

175

employees in the rue des Saussaies who maintained the heating and cleaned the lavatories. Could one of them know how to smuggle prisoners out of the building? And why me? What made me so extraordinary? Weren't there hundreds of arrests every day? Many detainees were shot without further ado. It seemed presumptuous to hope I wouldn't receive the standard treatment in this situation. Although I was bursting with questions, I put my ID tags back on. Henri hadn't expressed himself so curtly for nothing. *Tomorrow. Interrogation. Evening. Garden shed.*

I waited impatiently for the sounds that announced the evening meal, when the food cart stopped in front of the neighbouring cells. When the little window opened and I held out my bowl, I asked for a large portion. I wanted to be fortified for the following day. The old server, a trusty, wrinkled his forehead, but then he dipped the ladle a second time. I held the brimming bowl carefully and took slow spoonfuls, tasting for the various ingredients. Peas, some soft grain, a few chunks of rind. I chewed like someone who'd lost his teeth.

Next, I turned my attention to my eye. I'd protected it as well as I could while they were beating me. Carefully, I took the bandage off and touched the injured spot. I felt a scab and a moist pouch of what might have been pus. I shifted my eyes from side to side; the vision in my left eye was still blurred. I decided to take my chances without a bandage from now on. I lay down on the bed early and tried to sleep.

I came awake. There were noises outside in the corridor. The thought that they were coming to get me filled me with anticipation and fear. But it was someone else being brought in. I heard the detainee whimper and snuffle. At the end of the corridor, he screamed, but there was no way of making out what he said. I couldn't go back to sleep. A wheel of questions turned incessantly, round and round. Dawn was breaking when my head sank onto my chest.

I slept through breakfast. When I woke up, I was annoyed at myself for such negligence. I would need all my strength that evening. I tried doing push-ups on the stone floor. After three, I lay there on my chest, wretched and out of breath. Since nothing else could be done, I started walking again. I marched until it was time for the midday meal, after which I slept some more, lying on the plank bed, wearing my boots and my jacket. I wanted to be ready for anything. When night began to fall, I took the little piece of paper— Chantal's message—out of the straw mattress, read the lines with tender confidence, wrapped the paper around my nail, and threw it into the slop bucket. I was ready to leave my cell.

Nothing happened. The food cart with the evening meal came and went. Another hour passed. Work in the offices must have ended long since; they pulled night shifts only in the most urgent cases. I hauled myself up on the window bars and tried to see around the corner, but I couldn't pick out the window in my old department. Disappointed, I let myself drop, turned my back to the wall, and slid down to the floor. Where was Henri? I fell asleep sitting up.

*   *   *

177

Two days went by. Nothing unusual broke the daily routine. No one came to interrogate me, nor was there any sign of Henri, no matter how often I clicked my ID tags against the wall. I gave the food server questioning looks and ran to the peephole whenever footsteps approached. Thus I got myself into a state that consisted solely of uninterrupted waiting, which led me to do crazy things. I yanked off my boots because I felt a tiny fold in my sock that had to be smoothed out. I pulled myself up to the window and searched the opposite wall for *messages*. Then I brooded over whether or not Chantal had been caught. Why was she making me wait?

On the third night, I lay down on my bed early and stared at the ceiling like a man who was waiting to be hanged but didn't know what time the event would take place. And then—perhaps an hour later—I suddenly saw myself, in my prisoner pathos, as the epitome of wretchedness. My situation, my shattered nerves, meant only one thing: I was a miserable failure. I'd wanted to be *someone else*, to go for a walk *between* the lines—as a Frenchman, as a German, whichever I pleased. Leading Leibold by the nose, fooling the French— it had seemed so simple. What became clearest of all to me in those hours on my plank bed was this: I had believed there was no need for me to take up a position. I had just wanted to strip off the German and slip inside the Frenchman whenever I felt like it.

Never in my romantic euphoria had I wondered about Chantal's motives or taken into consideration the reasons that counted for her.

178

Now I saw that she had acted tactically from the first moment on. She'd played with me, delivered me into her people's hands, and later, although she recognized my infatuation, she hadn't hesitated to translate their plan into action. Chantal had always been engaged in the struggle, while I, tangled up in the idyll of my imaginings, had merely been fleeing reality. She'd kept the enemy in her sights while I was trying to shuttle back and forth between the lines. She'd gone into the whorehouse to kill the hated occupier. She'd *changed* something. All I'd changed were the terms of my comfort. I'd wanted to escape Reich and Führer, and so I fled to the Frenchman, to Monsieur Antoine. When he looked at me, I became the dull, stolid German, taking it easy on the banks of the Seine. Chantal had liked me; I no longer believed that she'd respected me. In her eyes, I was a chameleon, a man who yielded to any pressure, who was neither this nor that. There had been nothing heroic about my transformation into Monsieur Antoine; I was no daring charlatan, pulling a fast one on his own people. I was a coward who didn't dare make his opposition public. Leibold's brutish corporals were clearer about their convictions than I was about mine. In my arrogance and presumption, I had even hoped to be *freed*; I'd thought I could escape the people whose only remaining expense on my account would be for the bullet they were going to put in the back of my head.

That's what I was, and it was high time for me to realize it. There had never been an escape plan. There had never been an Henri. Whatever lay ahead for me, whether interrogation or

179

liquidation, I was resolved not to be taken in by promises again. When I finally fell asleep, I did so with the knowledge that I wasn't fooling myself anymore.

27

In the middle of the night, they came for me. They allowed me sufficient time to get properly dressed. Before we left the cell, I looked around, as though I dared not forget anything. We walked down the silent corridor. Many a prisoner was on the other side of his peephole, listening to our footsteps, happy that it was someone else and not himself who was being taken out. We went past the barbering room, past the doctor's station, and downstairs into the frigid courtyard. The open space was so white and bright, I thought at first it was illuminated by the moon, but in fact, the beam came from a large searchlight mounted on the roof ridge. A path shovelled through the snow lay in front of us. One SS soldier walked ahead of me, the other one behind, both of them sullen and weary.

I heard a buzz that seemed out of place in the soundless night. For a fraction of a second, I tensed my muscles and looked around. We'd reached the end of the courtyard, a little distance from the steps leading to Leibold's room. Beyond the steps was the garden shed, clearly visible in the garish light. The shed door—laths nailed to crosspieces—was slightly ajar. The padlock hung down at an angle, and the bolt was drawn back.

The buzzing ended in a detonation. The searchlight on the roof exploded. Voices and cries in the darkness. The sudden absence of light took all eyes by surprise. I sprang forward, shoved the leading SS private out of my way, charged into the deep snow, sank down, pumped my knees high, and bounded in the direction of the garden shed. Some contours grew visible again. Shouts of dismay from the privates, the sounds of safety catches being released. I collided with the wall of the shed, which I'd guessed was farther away. I could see enough to recognize the crack where the shed door stood open, and I stepped through it. I ran with my arms out in front of me and with no idea of what I was heading for. Gunshots struck the door, splintering the wood.

I banged into a wall, but then I found a passage that apparently led into the back building. Thick, persistent darkness. Groping my way along, I realized I'd entered a dwelling of some kind. Soft chairs, the outline of a fireplace. The next room was the kitchen; light shimmered in from the courtyard. I flinched when a figure appeared in the doorway.

'Vite, par ici,' a man said.

Approaching footsteps, coming the way I'd come. No time for questions. I followed him through the door, which he quickly locked behind us. Steps leading downward, damp walls; the beam from his flashlight ripped projecting stonework and electric wires from the darkness. The man hastened along ahead of me. We were in a ramifying system of cellars. At the end of a corridor, he came to a stop. Three steps mounted to a wooden door.

He shined the light on me. 'Might fit,' he said, throwing me a few pieces of clothing. A pair of shoes rolled toward me, as well.

'Who are you?' I gasped, getting out of my boots and unbuttoning my shirt.

'Quick, quick!'

Not a Parisian. He spoke like someone from the northern coast, perhaps Normandy. And there was something about the way he threw me the clothes. While I changed my shirt, I saw that the man had only one arm.

'Are you the gardener?'

He eyed me suspiciously. 'I know nothing about you, and you know nothing about me.'

'Did Henri set this up with you?'

'Get on with it!' he cried when I took too long to tie my shoe.

'Where am I supposed to go?' The jacket was too tight under the arms, and the pants were too big in the waist.

'I'm letting you out this door.'

'Where shall I hide?'

He stuck the key in the lock and shoved me up the steps. Cold night air. 'Good luck.'

'Do you have any money?'

The door was already closed. The key turned in the lock. The whole thing had lasted no more than two minutes, if that. Only now did I notice that I'd stopped hearing our pursuers. Quickly, I tried to get my bearings: I was in a side street not far from the church of La Madeleine. I could have reached the entrance to my former workplace by merely going around the corner. For a moment, I savoured the cold January night, breathed the air of freedom. But where could I go without papers

182

and without a centime in my pocket? I stepped out of the recess. The shoes were soft; I was doing the soft shoe right out of rue des Saussaies.

I quickly got a few blocks away and then stopped to listen; no hint of a search operation under way. I walked out of the neighbourhood unmolested and soon noticed that I was going toward my old hotel. A ridiculous habit. I paused in the shadow of a willow tree. I could think of only one place that seemed safe: the ruined entryway in the building near the horse butcher's shop, where I had undergone my *metamorphosis.*

My footsteps on the snowy streets. I had been ready for the shot in the back of the neck, the sudden flash, the sudden cooling; now I was making my way through silent Paris. No one had ever succeeded in escaping rue des Saussaies before. Who had made the arrangement with the one-armed gardener, and where had he disappeared to? Who had fired the shot that brought down the rescuing darkness?

I walked for half an hour, found the building, ran through the entryway into the courtyard, and slipped into the stairwell where my laundry bag used to await my return. I cleared away stones and brick fragments and crouched down. It wasn't so cold that I had to worry about freezing to death in my sleep. I was still warm from walking. I pulled my jacket tight around me, closed my eyes, and fell to thinking. Should I leave Paris? I'd be even more conspicuous in the country. The Germans were looking for me; the French wouldn't trust me. I didn't know where to find Chantal. Paris, then, I decided. I rejected any notion of crossing front lines and heading for home. From now on, I was a

183

wanted man, a deserter who could be shot without trial. The Allied invasion crossed my mind. I smiled. To hope that the war would change in a way useful to *me* seemed like the most extravagant of fantasies.

I fell asleep, awoke freezing, got up stiff-limbed, and warmed myself by walking in circles around the inner courtyard. I was hungry and thirsty. You have to think in simple terms, I told myself; think of the obvious. In the cold night, which wouldn't give way to morning, I felt my wounds most acutely. The wire in my jaw, my eye, which was leaking pus from one side, my bruises and lumps and cuts. I saw myself as a wreck. In rue des Saussaies, I'd taken my condition for granted. Now, however, in *freedom*, I was a pretty damaged specimen. In this state, I wouldn't be able to withstand much in the way of privation. As I was completing a circle, it came to me: Hirschbiegel. I had no idea what had happened to him after that night in Turachevsky's. He belonged to the Wehrmacht; his colonel was an influential man. No one would seriously suspect Hirschbiegel of having had anything to do with the attack. Was he still in Paris? Had his unit received its marching orders already? The warmer I got, the heavier my head felt. I crouched under the stairs and fell asleep again.

28

Quite early in the morning, shivering from head to toe, I set out for my old hotel. Officers and enlisted men were walking in and out of it continually. Since the Allied invasion was only a matter of time, two men with machine pistols patrolled in front of the entrance. A hundred metres farther on, I hid behind the trunk of an oak tree, hoping I'd be able to recognize Hirschbiegel despite the distance.

The clock in the church tower struck nine. Although he always went to work at 7:30, he still hadn't emerged. At ten o'clock, I turned away and headed for the river. Did it make any sense to wait in front of the building where Hirschbiegel's unit had its offices? Deep down, I knew the truth. If he wasn't staying in the hotel anymore, that meant he had left Paris. My friend was discharging his military obligation somewhere along the interminable Atlantic coast.

At noon, I reached Les Halles and got hold of some discarded vegetables. When a tumult erupted in the line of people waiting in front of a bakery, I seized the moment and stole a loaf of bread someone had dropped. That evening, I staked out the hotel a second time and tried again. But soon I realized my waiting was in vain.

As long as possible, I put out of my mind the idea of spending another night under the staircase. My dread of the cold was greater than my fear of being apprehended. As I wandered aimlessly through the second arrondissement and then the third, I noticed that I had inadvertently approached rue Faillard. I was seized by an insane hope that Hirschbiegel might have hidden the key somewhere. It was even possible that he'd figured I would show up at the flat one day. My longing to spend the night on that good mattress, in those comfortable rooms, was so irresistible that I resolved to risk the danger.

Moving cautiously, I turned into the narrow, empty street and stopped in front of the big door. I rang the bell and heard the familiar buzzing. My heart was racing as I stepped into the building and glided past the concierge's booth. By the time I reached the fourth floor, my knees were weak. Hunger and exhaustion. I sat down on the stairs and contemplated the door of the flat from the landing and considered where Hirschbiegel might have hidden a key. I felt along the door frame, stuck my fingers into recesses, looked under the mat. I examined the window and peered under the edges of the stair treads. I didn't want to admit the truth, so I went over everything twice. I crawled around, felt around, went down a floor and climbed back up, step by step, on my knees, left nothing out, and found nothing. In despair, I leaned all my weight on the door, but it didn't budge a millimetre. Now I saw how unfounded my fantasy was. Only a dreamer in the occupied city, where everybody sought to protect whatever he had, could have supposed that Hirschbiegel would leave a handy key stashed somewhere. But some good came of my efforts. I climbed the stairs to the attic door, curled up on the half landing, and spent at least that night with a roof over my head.

Strangely enough, in the following days I had no

fear of being recognized. The city was a prison in which inmates and guards tried to keep out of one another's way. Gradually, the prison began to seethe. Even though the season wasn't right, the Parisians took to wearing the three colours of the French flag. Red scarf, blue gloves, white shirt. Red coat, blue cap, white package under an arm. Despite the tightened security of those days, the painted *V* for Victory sign appeared on the walls of more and more buildings. The Wehrmacht, charged with obliterating the signs, could no longer keep up with them.

On my treks through the grey city, I observed dozens of prisoners. Few of them were Jews. Denunciations had increased; many people wanted to move quickly, before German rule came to an end, to rid themselves of a disagreeable neighbour or the proprietor of a competing shop. In spite of the frigid winter, Paris was edgier, more expectant, more aggressive than in the previous months. There were hours in which I saw myself not as an outcast, anathema to both sides, but as a normal figure amid the hustle and bustle. I came upon individuals in whom I recognized a fate like my own: exiles who had held on for three years in Paris and were now hoping for *libération.* Collaborators who felt their skin sloughing off and didn't know what new existence they should slip into. Most people were looking for something to eat. It seemed impossible to get hold of any hot food. Once I begged a bowl of soup from the Sisters of Mercy. Another time, the driver of a milk truck gave me some warm grog. Afterward, I stood foggy-brained on the Pont Royal and thought about the days when fishermen sat on the warm stone of this bridge.

Everybody dreamed about seeing the German uniforms disappear once and for all. They were, however, more present than ever. In every neighbourhood, at all the intersections, the occupiers acted with inflexible harshness. But the uprising was now a *thought*; it existed before the real preconditions for it had been established. I savoured being a nameless inhabitant of the city in those days. I was both observer and prisoner, united in one person.

29

A narrow track led through the snow. Rue de Gaspard lay there, grey and abandoned, not a living soul in sight. There must have been a fire in the junk dealer's shop. Black marks like tongues on the singed walls reached as high as the openings for the windows. A cold wind blowing. Old Joffo's bookshop was boarded up. I bent down and grabbed the corner of the lowest board. They'd done a thorough job, and they'd used long nails.

I retraced my steps. In front of the junk shop, I found a charred pole I could use as a lever. The first nail yielded with a screech; the board gave way a little. I pushed and pulled it, heedless of whether anyone was watching me. I ripped away two more planks and found the door handle. The glass had been shattered; I stuck my hand in and opened the door from inside. With a last look at the street, I crawled under the remaining boards and into the shop.

'Chantal!' I shouted as soon as I got past the door.

Everything had changed since the last time, when I'd found Joffo in the cellar. I looked around amid overturned bookshelves, smashed racks, and scattered books. Hundreds, thousands of volumes lay in heaps.

'Chantal, it's me!'

I was trembling with anticipation, but at the same time I was terrified at the thought of facing Chantal. I'd become pretty ragged since the last time we'd met; my trousers were dirty from sleeping on the ground, and many a loose thread hung from my jacket. My beard was unshaven and itchy. Earlier, when I passed in front of the Lubinsky, the waiter had failed to recognize me.

I worked my way deeper into the shop, reached the counter, and slipped around it. Pensively, I picked up Joffo's ledger. My eyes scanned the little figures—I caught myself adding them up. I put the book aside and moved to the stove, where the poker was. My fingers sought out its flattened tip; weeks ago, I'd used this tool to raise the trapdoor. I pried it open again, just as I'd done before, lighted a match, and climbed down into the cellar.

'Chantal!' I repeated her name several times. 'Don't hide, Chantal! Chantal, it's me!'

Everything in the cellar was as I remembered it: dirty, empty, and forsaken. I lit up every corner. There was a bucket of old potatoes on the floor, their shoots intertwined with one another. The match burned my fingers. I dropped it and then just stood there, weary with disappointment.

The idea had come to me earlier, under the

189

arches of the Pont Royal: Chantal hadn't left Paris! She was hiding—just like me! It had seemed like the only possible explanation. I went back up to the shop, sat down on a mound of books, and took my head in my hands.

'On the day when the Germans marched into Paris, Papa accompanied old Bertrand to the Champs-Élysées.'

Chantal was wearing the same heavy jacket she'd had on the last time I saw her in Turachevsky's. Mannishly, she put one foot on the books and braced her elbows against her knee. 'The two old fellows stood on the side of the street, not saying a word,' she continued. 'To keep from crying, Papa said, he sang the "Marseillaise" under his breath. The tank treads were making so much noise, no one heard him.'

'And then?'

'Bertrand started singing the "Internationale." Imagine it—two old men, singing, and the German panzers rolling by.'

She pushed her hair off her forehead. My side itched. Even though it seemed ungentlemanly to do so in Chantal's presence, I started scratching myself. I'd picked up a flea somewhere. He was making himself comfortable in the warmth of my armpits.

'A year later, in the rue de Seine, I found a leaflet and brought it home,' she said. 'Papa read it with a degree of emotion he ordinarily reserved for the works of Rabelais.'

Now that I'd started, I couldn't stop scratching. I hunched my shoulders and scraped and rubbed and did a jerky dance. This didn't bother Chantal.

'Soon after that, Gustave came back from the

190

front. He brought a Gascon with him. A man with the necessary contacts. That same week, we carried the individual parts of a printing press, piece by piece, into the cellar under the barbershop.'

The itching was getting even worse. I jumped up, scratching harder and harder. Something stuck to the sole of my shoe—a bit of coloured paper. I raised my leg, scratching it the whole time, and glanced at the paper; it was a drawing. I pulled it off my shoe. Simple lines, the spaces between them filled in with coloured pencils. I recognized at once what the picture represented: 'The Fox and the Grapes.'

'Did you draw this, Chantal?' I asked. Chantal went into the shop. I looked at the drawing, which showed the fox with his forepaws on a tree trunk. The branch with the cluster of grapes was out of his reach.

'Have you ever wondered,' I cried out, 'why the artist hangs the grapes on a tree, when they actually grow on vines?' I imagined Chantal as a child, sitting here with her pencils and copying the illustrations in the book. 'All roads are in the *Fables*,' I murmured. Then I raised my head and listened.

'What did you mean by that—'All roads are in the *Fables*'?' I followed Chantal into the shop. 'Chantal?'

I carefully folded the paper and put it in my pocket. Then I started stalking around like a bookworm gone mad, picking up something here, smoothing out a creased page there. I tried to reconstruct the way the books had once been arranged. I found a shelf with *R* and *S* and stepped

191

across to the opposite wall, where Baudelaire had been cast down, along with the other authors whose names started with *B*. I raised overturned bookcases and dug into the heaps of books, throwing aside the ones whose authors' names didn't begin with *F*. Stopping often so I could listen, I finally found Flaubert. Then I started digging harder, until all at once I was looking at the familiar cover illustration: sea green water, and in the depths the shadowy fish-monster. I carefully picked up the volume of La Fontaine's *Fables*. 'Yes,' I said, nodding in the fading indoor light. 'Yes indeed!' I sat on a prostrate bookcase and started turning pages.

'The Dove and the Ant.'

'The Astrologer Who Fell into a Well.'

'The Hare and the Frogs.'

I read excitedly, with one finger on the pictures. When I came to the fable of 'The Cock and the Fox,' I stopped. In the margin, there was a copy of a detail from the illustration. A childish hand had drawn Doré's fox in pencil.

'You have talent, Chantal,' I said, smiling and concentrating even harder on the following pages. Soon I started discovering not only pictures in the margins but also annotations. Next to the picture of a dire wolf, I deciphered the words 'Uncle Bébert.' And 'When we were in Trouville' was scribbled beside a seascape.

I reached the fable called 'Fortune and the Young Boy.' Fortuna, a strapping nude, stands on the wheel of fortune with one hand on a little boy's breast. He's sitting on the edge of a well; thick vegetation surrounds them both. I recognized the picture—it had been the first female nude of my childhood. On the lower margin of the page, some pencilled words: 'Grandpa's woods, forest of Balleroy.'

I sat motionless, staring at the phrase, and recollected Chantal's words. The first time we met, she called the fish on the cover a 'catfish.'

'Where can you catch catfish?' I asked.

'My grandfather catches them sometimes. In the country.'

I stood up slowly and laid the open book on the counter. The forest of Balleroy. I started looking around again. After a while, I was holding a school atlas in my hand. It had been published during the previous war, but I figured that the place names could hardly have changed.

'Balleroy,' I said. 'Where's Balleroy, Chantal?'

At first, I searched in the vicinity of Paris, and then I turned to the northern regions and departments—Ile-de-France and Seine-et-Marne, followed by Picardie, Val-d'Oise, and Haute-Normandie. My eyes gradually began to burn from reading the tiny print on the map. The farther west I searched, the more improbable it seemed that I'd find Balleroy. The Joffos weren't Normans; it wasn't likely that the family would have property up in Normandy. I made a new search, this time starting south of Paris, but I didn't find any place named Balleroy.

The light disappeared. I'd stayed there much too long! My carelessness gave me a fright. Hastily scooping up the *Fables* and the atlas, I slipped out of the shop, protected by the gathering twilight. While I pressed the boards back into place, I looked around. Chantal wasn't waiting for me anywhere.

I reached rue Jacob. The folding grille had been let down in front of the barbershop. The Jewish haberdasher had given up his shop, too. I avoided German patrols as much as I could and made my way back to my sleeping place. I turned into rue Faillard under cover of darkness, pressed the books against my body, and ran past two automobiles to the building's entrance. The big door buzzed open. I stepped gingerly along the entryway and drew near the concierge's booth.

The make of the two parked automobiles burst upon my consciousness. It was too late. I already heard the footsteps; two men were running after me. The door of the little booth slowly opened. I tried to stop, skidded on the slick stones, bounced back. Leibold was standing in front of me. His cap was at the correct angle, the top two buttons of his overcoat properly fastened. He slapped his gloves against his thigh. In the silence, which seemed to me interminable, I asked, 'How did you find me?'

'I hadn't ever lost you.' His smile was unusually cheerful. 'Not for a moment.'

He was only two steps away from me. All at once, I felt hot. Images flashed across my mind. The one-armed gardener in rue des Saussaies who had shown no fear whatsoever of our pursuers. The SS soldiers who were hot on our heels and then suddenly disappeared. Why weren't my suspicions aroused when I saw that Joffo's shop wasn't under surveillance? And I'd rummaged around in there for more than an hour. Shouldn't I have realized what Hirschbiegel would say to his interrogators after the attack in Turachevsky's? That he would at the very least give up the secret of rue Faillard? I understood that the previous weeks hadn't been *lucky*; they'd been Leibold's plan. He'd let me swim around like a goldfish in a bowl, watching me the whole time. The freedom I'd enjoyed had been a favour to me from Leibold. He'd waited patiently until I went back to the bookshop and discovered what he couldn't find: Chantal's location.

An SS corporal stepped out from behind Leibold, his weapon at the ready.

I had no hope and not the slightest chance. But nevertheless, I sprang forward, grabbed Leibold by the arms, and shoved him into the corporal. For a moment, I felt the bandage on his back. The corporal couldn't shoot without hitting Leibold. Both of them staggered backward; the smile vanished from Leibold's face.

'Don't,' he said crossly.

I ran. The others' steps were so close behind me, I figured I'd be granted the coup de grâce any moment now. Holding the books with both hands—why were there no shots?—I dashed up the first flight of stairs and then the second. Apparently, they wanted me alive. There was no escape for me anywhere. My breathing grew loud. I leaped up three steps at a time; from below me came the sound of hobnailed boots, in no hurry.

I'd made the discovery three nights before. The weak spot in the wall, the sabotaged spot. The padlock on the attic door was massive and solid. But its frame was pegged into crumbly masonry. I'd hoped that a certain amount of effort would enable me to lever the peg out of the wall and get into the attic. I'd used a sharp-edged piece of scrap iron as a tool and scraped away for hours during each of the last few nights.

195

The sound of Leibold's voice issuing orders mingled with the stamping noise of the boots. I ran past Wasserlof's flat. I was certain it had been gone through quite thoroughly. Soon I stood before the iron door, panting openmouthed and yanking on the lock. The metal frame didn't budge. I pressed my fingers underneath it and tore at it in a frenzy. The peg moved a millimetre and then sprang back. I pulled on it and heard Leibold and his men reach the third floor. I bent lower and the books fell to the floor. I groped for the piece of scrap iron and rammed it between the wall and the frame. Sharp edges cut into the balls of my fingers. I levered like a madman, screamed in desperation—and suddenly the frame was in my hand. Blood. There wasn't enough time to pick up both books, so I grabbed the nearest one and stumbled into the dark. Shouts from down below; they'd found my escape route. I closed my eyes in the total darkness, then opened them again and saw the rectangular outline of the skylight, dim against a black background. I shoved the book down the front of my trousers, buttoned my jacket over it, and hurried over to the skylight. The lock was high up and rusted shut. I had no choice but to ram the glass window with my head. At first, the glass cracked, and then the skylight burst; glass shards rained down on my shoulders. I bent the wooden frame backward. The SS soldiers reached the attic door; the beams from their flashlights danced.

I stuck my arms out into the open air above my head, gathered myself, and jumped. Although I was out of breath and there was hardly anything in my stomach, I had enough strength to pull myself up. I thrust my shoulders out, heaved myself higher, and hung for a moment between heaven and earth. Then, quickly clearing my legs, I rolled onto the steep-pitched roof, held on to the skylight frame, and looked around. Only a thin layer of snow covered the shingles, but I could feel ice beneath it. I clambered up.

Now there were shots; they were firing through the roof. One of them shone his light through the opening and shot into the night. I saw the flash from his weapon and felt the bullet hiss past me. I scrambled higher, clawed the shingles, slid back, kicked out, and at last grabbed the round ridge of the roof. Drawing in my breath with a shriek, I pulled myself up the rest of the way, straddled the crest, and scooted along on the seat of my pants. My pursuer's head turned in my direction; he fired. Two bullets whizzed past me, but the third one found its mark and tore through my ribs. I crumpled over, toppling onto the other side of the roof. There was a dormer window, a projection of some sort, maybe a ledge. As my side started to burn, I let go and slid down on my shoulder. The adjoining roof, coming in at a corresponding angle, slowed my fall, but I couldn't grasp anything. I slid past raised, snowy roof tiles, grabbing at them wildly while my feet thrashed about, looking for traction. Ice everywhere. I seized a hook—briefly—and felt a hot stabbing in my hand. Something tore. I shot out over the gutter and caught hold of the thin metal at the last second. It cracked and started to come apart. I held on tightly, as though the gutter were a flying carpet. Even this last handhold was ripped away from me. For a long moment, I was completely

197

free in the blackness. Happy to have escaped them, to have flown away into the night.

30

The eyes of the Virgin Mary. Also a dim reddish light. I wasn't really awake. Only groaning. Consciousness disappeared again.

Later, lying on my side, I felt warmth on my back. Soft watery sounds. Someone was washing me. A powerful forearm, a broad figure bent over my body, curly hair. The shape held still and looked at me.

'So you're really there,' a woman's voice said.

Unable to move. I was a sigh, nothing more. I heard quiet laughter. Water ran along my back. Time.

Languid, drowsy, dozing; I didn't want to wake up. I was able to perceive but not to discern. The room and the sounds seemed close. Someone came and went. Above me, a picture on the wall: *La Vierge Marie.* A figure dressed in blue, standing in a pleasant garden. The first world I saw. Looking serious, God's mother pointed upward, but the top part of the picture lay in shadow. I tried to imagine a dove.

Had I moved? The person in the room stood still, wiped her hands, came closer.

'Are you awake? Are you awake?'

I turned my eyes away from the Virgin. Pain grabbed me and shook my whole body.

'No. You've still got a long way to go,' the woman said.

She bent lower. She was older but by no means elderly. Her eyes weren't merry, her nose was flat, and only her mouth smiled. Dark hair with grey streaks. A blue apron dress of some soft fabric.

'I don't have anything to help your pain,' she said. 'Nothing at all.' She pointed to me.

No strength to lift my head and look at myself. My body must have been shattered. Two pieces of wood ran along my right arm, starting at the shoulder. Splints made of boards. They gently knocked against each other. Around my left hand, a thick bandage.

'I'm no doctor.' She shifted the splinted arm to a different position. 'There isn't any doctor. You have to eat something.' The pain was dull and distant.

'I wonder if you've still got *one* sound bone in your body,' she said. Her hand moved toward my hair. 'You have to eat,' she declared, stressing the words. 'You understand me?'

I wasn't wearing anything that could tell her where I came from. How did she know I wasn't French?

'You're the crazy *boche*.' She straightened her back. 'Look, I know that much.' My eyes questioned her.

'I'm the concierge. My name is Valie.'

I jumped. Leibold had come out of the concierge's booth. He'd been lurking in there, waiting for me.

She noticed the fright in my eyes. 'At first, I hid you in the cellar. The building's four hundred years old. The cellar has a cellar even older than that. They looked for you the whole night and all the next day. They'll probably come again.' She

199

followed my eyes to the picture of the Virgin Mary. 'Now we're somewhere else.'

Suddenly, she smiled. 'I saw you go up to the flat with the young lady. You two went up there twice.' She said these words as though they contained a great mystery.

'I know the Wasserlof flat,' she went on as she stood up. 'Why doesn't the young lady go there anymore?' When I didn't answer, she left the room. 'You'll tell me all about it sometime.'

I listened to my breathing. She'd called me a *boche*. She was hiding me. She'd managed to conceal me from the search teams. Was this another of Leibold's traps? Where was the room I was in? The building? My staying here seemed as unreal to me as the time I'd spent unconscious. Where had I landed when I fell?

I uttered a sound. She came back. It took me a long time to form the word: 'Today.'

She leaned forward. 'It's the beginning of February. The sixth, I believe.'

She smiled at the moan that escaped me. 'Yes, you've been down a long time. You were dead, believe me. Dead. All you had left was a little spark. You were all smashed up, but you didn't let the little spark go out. You're tough, *boche*. Now let me go and warm your soup.' She disappeared from sight.

The concierge fed me. She put the end of a little metal funnel in my mouth. I wanted to bite down on it, but I couldn't. I thought the wire in my jaw was broken, but I noticed that I was missing a couple of teeth on the left side. Valie carefully poured soup into the funnel. The liquid ran down from the corners of my mouth. When she moved

200

the funnel to the right, things went better. I drank and swallowed, savouring the warmth.

'You still can't bite,' she said. 'But it looks like you can swallow all right.' She smiled. 'So not everything in there is broken.'

I listened to my insides, trying to follow the path of the soup.

31

Gradually, I started to believe I'd escaped death. Days and weeks passed, during which the only changes were trivial. Daphne blooms appeared on Valie's chest of drawers and then were taken away. One afternoon, the sun was so bright it lit up the whole picture of the Madonna. There actually was a dove hovering over her, surrounded by the symbol of the Holy Trinity. I contemplated the sunlit picture until the light disappeared again, centimetre by centimetre.

In this period, Chantal didn't visit me even once. In my daydreams, I imagined her as a warrior, dressed in dark trousers, her hair pinned up under her cap. She knew how to handle weapons. I rarely saw her in her light green dress. She said nothing; she only sat there on the bed or walked past it. It became clearer and clearer to me that Chantal couldn't have known anything. She'd never learned of my arrest. Therefore, she hadn't sent me any secret messages. Ultimately, I accepted the notion that Henri had been a kind of tapping poltergeist that Leibold had put in my head. I'd gone reeling through the Parisian winter on *his* behalf.

One morning, I asked the concierge, more with gestures than with words, to bring me my books. She gave me the one I'd stuck in my pants before going off the roof. It wasn't the *Fables*. They'd probably fallen into Leibold's hands and were gone for good. The open atlas lay on my stomach. Valie sat next to me, turning the pages and looking at maps of the poles, the configurations of Oceania and Southeast Asia. Since I could move neither arms nor hands, I asked her to turn to France. France: post-1918 boundaries. Cities, rivers, regions.

I was looking for a short, simple name. Something regal was hidden in it. The word began with an *F* or a *B*. I was sure it would come back to me. The village, the hamlet, where Chantal's grandfather's property was—the place whose name she'd scribbled in the margin of the *Fables*. Every day, I spent hours trying to recall that name. My eyes slid over the various towns. I didn't want to admit to myself that I had, inexplicably, forgotten it.

Valie brought me soup—vegetable soup, mostly. Once, she dipped bits of white bread in milk and put it in my mouth piece by piece. I chewed it with my gums and the stumps of my remaining teeth. How good it tasted! From that day on, she brought me bread soup every day.

I often thought about how I could properly thank Valie for taking care of me. However, my suspicion that she might be working for Leibold had not vanished altogether. When my face had healed to the point where I could speak, I asked her, 'Why are you doing this for me?'

Valie was sitting on the stool next to my bed. It

was evening.

'I knew Wasserlof,' she said. Her hands lay motionless on her apron. 'One day, he arrived with a lady and gentleman from Germany and showed them the apartment. Monsieur and Madame Hirschbiegel were elegant people. Monsieur gave me something for my trouble.'

She stood up and rummaged about the room. 'After that, he often came to Paris alone, even after Wasserlof died. When the Germans marched in, I asked him, 'What's going to happen with the flat?' He said, 'I guess I'm not going to get around to painting it.' That made us both laugh.' Valie's cheeks glowed. 'One day, well into the war, Hirshbiegel's son showed up to try out his key. He doesn't look like his father. Then you and the young lady came. In the end, the Germans came.' Valie shrugged her shoulders. 'That's it.'

I didn't understand her cheerfulness. She was talking about the enemy, after all. Hirschbiegel was a Wehrmacht lieutenant. I myself was the enemy who'd occupied the city and had his fun with a Parisian girl. I asked Valie about this. She only smiled and left the room without answering.

She was in her middle forties and rather pretty, in a ripe, ponderous way. Even in her apron dress, there was something attractive about her. I'd often wanted to ask her where her husband was. Had he been killed in combat or taken prisoner? All I found out was that Valie had worked as a nurse before the war. She knew a few things about bones.

She wasn't worried about my right leg. The break in my femur had been clean and was healing normally. In my left leg, however, both bones had been splintered, and my calf was a mess. Valie cleaned the open wounds and put the broken parts back together. So far, there had been no infection. But whether the leg was growing back together in the correct position, she couldn't say.

The wood and bandages I was wrapped with began to smell. She changed the splints. I hardly felt anything. Except for a few bruises, my left arm was almost healed, so I could eat and leaf through the school atlas reasonably well. The sole hindrance was the bandage on my hand. I'd seen the wound under the dressing only once. Valie prepared me for the shock: my little finger had been torn off at the joint. It must have happened when I skidded off the roof. The skin was beginning to close over the bones. The place itched, but no worse than a wasp sting.

In the beginning of March, the fever came. At first, the spot under my knee looked like a boil. Then it began to fester. The skin swelled and burst and white fluid came out. Valie cleaned the wound daily with chamomile tea. I was in a lot of pain, and my whole body trembled. My blood raced; I thought I was going to lose my reason. Every time I opened my eyes, time had jumped ahead. I had no dreams, except one.

It began on a slope, where I was riding a bicycle downhill. I was surprised that the bike didn't find the way down by itself. It was heavy. I looked at it more closely; it was made of pure gold. Immediately, the bicycle turned into a perfectly round crown with large points. With an effort, I pushed it in front of me, farther and farther down the hill. Where to? I thought. What's down there? Finally, I reached the lowest point, and there was

204

the sea. I understood: The crown had to go into the water. I rolled it on in.

When I woke up, a word was with me. The word that belonged to the crown. *Balleroy.* I raised my head. 'Balleroy,' I said to the Virgin Mary. She pointed upward.

When Valie came, I asked her if she knew a town named Balleroy, perhaps a place on the sea. She tried to wipe my forehead and cool my wrists. I warded her off and asked for the atlas. Hesitantly, she opened it to the map of France. I wasn't strong enough to concentrate very long. Everything got blurry. Soon, I fell asleep.

The next morning, Valie put a sharp knife in boiling water, took the knife out of the pot with a cloth, bent over my leg, and made an incision below my knee. I screamed. A great deal of liquid matter flowed out of the cut. Valie cleaned the wound with brandy. I lost consciousness.

After I came to, I asked her to join me in searching the map. She moved the stool beside the bed. We began in the north, on the Belgian border, and travelled south and east along the coast. At frequent intervals, I repeated the name Balleroy. We moved through the *départements* bordering the English Channel: Pas-de-Calais, Somme, Seine-Maritime, Eure. In Calvados, our fingers passed over the bathing resorts of Saint-Laurent-sur-Mer and Arromanches-les-Bains and investigated the area around Caen and Bayeux. And all at once, just as we were about to move on to Cherbourg, there was the name, right in front of us. Valie put her finger under it, and I said it. It was in small print, but clearly legible: Balleroy.

It was in Basse-Normandie, much farther from

Paris than I had assumed. The road that led there was a very thin line on the map. Somewhere along that road was Chantal's grandfather's farm. Maybe you won't die after all, I said to myself. From that moment on, there was *conviction* in me.

The season of the year added to my confidence. As my infection gradually faded away, spring began. Even in the dark room, where sunlight never stayed long, you could feel nature waking up. I didn't want to be sick anymore. Something had to change!

While I was still bedridden, listening to my splints knock together every time I shifted a leg, the trip to Normandy began to take shape in my mind. I could see it so clearly, it seemed as if rue Faillard led directly to the Balleroy road. Valie felt my restlessness and forgave my frequent whining. I was a disagreeable, ill-humoured patient who wanted out. I hated lying there, and I tried to get Valie to help me stand up. I asked for my clothes so often, she laid out shirt and trousers on the chair. From now on, they were ready, like a prospect of things to come.

Valie brought me scissors; my beard hung down to my chest. I cut off clumps of curly hair. When Valie came in with a shaving brush and a razor and went calmly to work, I was certain she'd had a man and shaved him in such a way. Sitting amid beard clippings, I asked her about this.

'Yes, there was someone,' she said. 'But he won't ever come back.'

'Why not?'

'He's far away.' The blade scraped over my cheek.

'Is he in the war somewhere?'

'He's not well.'

'Wounded?'

She spoke hesitantly, but her voice was full of longing. 'All I know is that Herr Hirschbiegel had to be admitted to a Munich hospital. His wife wrote and told me. That was before the war.'

Pensively, unhurriedly, Valie told me the story of her love affair with her German gentleman, which had lasted for many years. Since the letter from his wife, Valie had had no further news of him. She didn't know whether monsieur was still alive.

I'd attributed many different motives to her, but not this one. While the blade passed over my chin and my throat, Leibold's phantom, which had always lurked behind Valie, disappeared at last.

She gave me back my real face. At my insistence, she brought a mirror. It was a ghastly sight. The SS corporals' *techniques* had fixed my jaw so that it hung down sideways. My lower teeth were exposed, the gaps between them clearly visible. They'd broken my nose; the smooth, narrow ridge was now a bumpy outcrop. I must have injured my neck when I fell—I had a scar from my ear to my collarbone. In many spots on my skull, the hair had been replaced by scabs; sparse tufts were growing back here and there. I'd lost weight, my forehead was deeply lined, and purple bags hung down under my eyes. My twenty-third birthday wasn't far off. But the person gazing at me from the mirror looked a lot older than that.

We took the splint off my right leg. The break had to be healed by now. I pushed my leg off the bed, laid my arm around Valie's shoulders, set my foot on the floor, and stood up. I'd figured on being very weak, but the truth was horrifying. My leg folded up like a lifeless piece of meat. I sensed the floor tile under the ball of my foot and felt my knee bend, but the leg was useless. I almost fell over. Valie held me up. She began hauling me around the room. The still-splinted leg served as a support; I dragged the other one along. We went in a circle. I was much too heavy for her, and soon she was breathing hard. After a few minutes, she dragged me back to the bed. I was despondent at the thought that I'd have to stay there several more weeks.

I asked Valie for other books, and she promised to get me some. That very evening, she brought me a German novel. It looked familiar. After some hemming and hawing, she admitted to having taken the book from Hirschbiegel's flat. She had a key.

'You mean I could use it, too?' I asked enthusiastically.

'What's the matter, you don't like my place anymore, *boche*?' It was the first time she'd used the word as a slur.

32

Many weeks had passed since I'd fallen from the roof into Valie's keeping. I was a shattered man, and she nursed me; I was a wanted man, and she hid me. How could I repay her? One evening, leafing through the atlas again, I noticed a page had come away from the binding. It was of the South Pacific and Oceania, detached from the rest of the world. For several minutes, I studied islands with such names as Onotoa or Nanumaga and ran my finger along the perimetre of the Fiji Basin. I followed the trace of the international date line, east of which it was always a day later than it was west of the line. Eventually, I picked up the loose page, smoothed it, and began to fold it. I had to destroy my creation twice, but on the third try, I succeeded in making a bird. Both of its wings were blue. Its head was formed by the New Zealand coastline; the Gilbert Islands decorated its tail. I wrote 'For Valie' on its underside and waited for evening to come.

'A farewell gift?' she asked.

I was eating bean stew. She sat on the stool next to the bed and looked at the paper creature in her lap.

'How do you expect to make it?' My bird, like a swan unfit for flight, flew awkwardly from her hand.

'The way I've made it up to now,' I replied, hastening over the route in my mind.

Landscapes in the first flush of spring. Trees laden with blooms, the green haze over the fields. It was the end of March. I knew they'd assigned a quarter of a million men to the reinforcement of the Atlantic Wall. Ten bunkers per kilometre of shoreline. Dunkerque, Le Havre, Cherbourg, Saint-Malo, Brest, and the Channel Islands had been declared 'fortresses.' Panzer units, assault-gun units, and tank-destroyer units had moved in. Most of the soldiers were stationed in the very region I intended to cross.

On a crutch, alone, without money or papers. Searching for Chantal.

Valie thanked me and left the room. I lay awake

209

all night long, imagining what would happen. I hoped Chantal could hear me.

*   *   *

The splint was bound tightly to my lower leg, over my trousers. We embraced; I patted Valie's warm back and felt the deep breath of the woman to whom I owed my life. It was unlikely that we'd ever see each other again. And yet Valie and I spoke about a time 'afterward' and made a plan to meet when everything was over. With the crutch jammed into my armpit, I opened the door. We didn't kiss. As I hobbled out onto rue Faillard, the wooden shafts made loud stumping sounds on the pavement.

I slipped out of the city by the morning light, in a group of about a hundred men on their way to join a labour deployment. Once I was past the Bois, I hitched a ride in a vegetable truck. The driver asked no questions. I was wearing a brown suit and shoes with hobnailed soles, because Valie had assumed that I'd have to travel most of the way on foot. She'd even managed to rustle up a coat for me.

Luck abandoned me after Poissy. A cloudburst made the road, which German tanks had turned into a gravelly wasteland, impassable; the truck got stuck. The driver and I tried using boards to give the vehicle some traction. That was how I ruined my suit the first day I wore it. When the rain slackened, the vegetable man set out for the village to fetch a yoke of oxen. We bade each other farewell, and I continued my journey on foot. I hadn't managed to travel very far from Paris.

210

The crutch sank into the muddy ground. I spent the first night by a stream, in the shelter of a willow grove. I drank water and ate some of the provisions that Valie had packed for me. Even though I was cold, it was an amazing experience to lie on the ground under a stormy sky after weeks cooped up in a back room. I closed my eyes euphorically and tried to recall what I knew about edible plants and mushrooms and berries, until it occurred to me that I wasn't going to find anything of that sort in early April. All the same, I knew I'd reach Balleroy in the end, no matter how long it took. I imagined Chantal's surprise, her happiness. I'd wait with her for the end of the war, work in the fields, and help with the harvests until we could begin our new lives.

The next morning, endless columns of troop carriers came rolling down the road. None of the men in the flatbed trucks paid any attention to the cripple on the roadside. Nevertheless, I decided that from now on I'd travel only on cross-field paths and cart tracks. For reference, I'd torn the map of northern France out of the atlas.

On the second evening, in a village named Thière, I determined that I'd covered only a few kilometres, and that I'd gone too far to the south. Exhausted and discouraged, I crawled into a barn, lay down on my coat, and piled hay on myself. I awoke freezing in the dark, pulled on my coat, and burrowed deeper into the hay.

The weather changed. It became clammy and capricious, and the nights were frigid. If I slept outside, in the morning my suit was covered with frost. I'd gone through all my victuals in three days. I didn't like the idea of stealing.

In those days, there were lots of dubious riffraff on the roads, people like me. Wherever I went, I encountered suspicion. No one invited me to share a meal or voluntarily provided me with a place to spend the night. After making the acquaintance of my third farm dog, which pursued me to the end of its chain, I started simply taking what I needed— stealing chunks of stale bread from horse troughs, tearing the first spring onions out of the earth and eating them raw. Sometimes I roasted bread and onions together on a wooden spat. Once a farmer smelled my campfire and ran me off with a couple of shotgun blasts. By that time, I was able to hump along on my crutch so nimbly that not even men with two healthy legs could keep up with me.

I'd never milked a cow in my life. After a few tries, I was able to do it even in the dark. I knew how to soothe the beasts and how to avoid their hooves. When a whole farmstead was asleep, I'd sneak into the chicken coop and steal the hens' eggs. One night, I even dared to climb into an open farmhouse window. I unbolted the smoking chamber and grabbed a chunk of bacon. The farmer's dog started yapping so close beside me that I dropped the bacon and ran off. Afterward, I was angry with myself. What was a bite on the leg compared with the enjoyment of some tasty pork belly?

After a particularly frigid night—I'd been on the road for nearly three weeks by then—I woke up with chills and fever, which forced me to remain all that day on my back in the hay. I had to wait there for three days, which meant three days without any nourishment. On the fourth morning, I woke up well again. Feeling the spring in my limbs, I clambered down from the hayloft and went outside to warm myself in the sun.

Since there was no longer any doubt that the Allies would invade, the Germans weren't concentrating so hard on the enemy within. Most matters between the French and the occupying forces sorted themselves out. The reciprocal moratorium was broken only by partisan attacks and the reprisals that followed them. I hadn't seen any firing-squad executions myself, but a baker's wife told me the story of an entire hamlet whose population was exterminated because two German soldiers on a motorcycle had been blown up.

I continued to avoid fortified roads. I'd assumed I wouldn't meet the first units until I got close to the sea, and I was surprised by the colossal scale of the troop movements that were taking place. I saw tanker trucks for panzer divisions, personnel carriers, and armoured tank transports loaded with steel scaffolding a metre long. I passed freshly levelled roads, saw bridges that had been blown up to impede the enemy's advance into the interior. Hobbling on my crutch, I skirted fields mined by German sappers and circumvented checkpoints, if I noticed them in time. I luckily got past one by shouldering my crutch like a shovel and joining a work gang.

Near a place called Heudebouville, I investigated a solitary farm. I caught only a brief glimpse of part of the family: an older farm couple, five or six children, two farmworkers. Farming people almost always went to bed with the chickens, but there the lights stayed on long after nightfall. I gazed at them from my observation post behind a tree and heartily wished I'd be able to crawl into the hay soon. The dog was a blustery old woofer who barked for no reason. His people hardly paid him any attention.

Finally, the last window grew dark. I crept to the barn door and opened it just wide enough to slip through. The dog whimpered. I climbed a ladder to the threshing floor, spread out my coat, and covered myself with as much hay as I could reach. My eyes closed at once.

The sky was dark. Shouts woke me up, but I didn't understand the language right away. Just as I was crawling toward the wooden wall, the racket began. A breaking window. Footsteps and screams in the house. Somewhere a door was smashed in. Crying children, scolding voices. Through an opening in the wall, I saw torches and flashlights. There was a shot and a pitiful outcry. Beams of light playing over the straw, flickering dust particles, torn from the darkness. More shouts.

'Here's another one!'

A leather coat, a grey cap. I was wide awake and dazed at the same time. Unable to move, I had but one thought: Gestapo.

'Down the ladder.' The language the man spoke wasn't German; it was the local dialect. His pistol was an old model. When I reached for my crutch, he fired. I cried out in mortal fright and pointed to the splint on my leg. The man found the crutch and threw it to the floor below. I limped to the ladder, climbed down carefully, and stepped into the open. I'd forgotten my coat.

Standing at the barn gate, I could see ten men, Frenchmen, driving the family together. Flames leapt up behind a window. The grandmother and the farmer's wife were with the small children; the

214

older boys, intimidated and half-asleep, pressed around the father. One of the workers squatted down, looking dazed; the other was just being brought in. I couldn't completely shake off my sleepiness, and I felt a sickly, debilitating fear. I was shoved forward, hands clasped behind my head. I didn't understand what was happening. The armed men were French; their regional speech was the same as the farmers'.

The big farmer, wearing underpants and a fleece jacket, was led to the manure pile. An order was bawled out; two soldiers aimed and fired. The women's screams came as though from one throat. While the victim's heavy body was still sinking to the ground, his father was brought in. He clambered stiff-legged over his son's corpse. The women stopped screaming; the children stood and gaped wide-eyed. The elderly man expired with a sigh. Next it was the older worker's turn. He fought and bellowed. A bullet struck him in the temple.

Now the man in the cap shoved me toward the manure heap. As my hands were still raised, I lost my balance and fell. On the ground, I found the smell of the dung surprisingly intense. I was pulled to my feet and hustled past the women. Looks of amazement—nobody knew me. There was hardly room to stand among the dead. Not a sound. I turned around and tried to speak, but all I managed to get out was a croak. The other farmworker was hauled up at my side. In the torchlight, three men aimed their weapons. I saw an outstretched hand pointing at the man next to me. His muscles tensed. When I heard the shot, the worker was already sinking down, his hand raised as though in defence. The whispering sound was my own breath. Everything was silent. They reloaded and raised the rifle butts to their shoulders.

'No,' someone said.

He was young. His shirt had a torn collar; and he was the only one not carrying a weapon. He took a few steps toward me but didn't climb over the bodies. He was hardly older than I was; his eyeglasses gave him a winsome look. He looked me up and down.

'You're not from around here,' he said.

'No.' I looked back at him.

'Who are you?'

'They burned down my village,' I said softly.

'Where?'

Everyone waited for my answer. It would determine whether I lived or died. Someone had told me the name of a place the Germans had destroyed. I couldn't think of it. I let my hands fall, staggering on my injured leg.

'What's the name of the village?' he asked without impatience.

I let my head droop; I simply couldn't say anything. I started to cry. Two men came up, escorting the farmer's oldest son.

'These are traitors,' the man with the glasses said, as though I had the right to an explanation before the execution was carried out. 'Collaborators. Also informers, and therefore sentenced to death.'

He made sure I had understood. Then, in conclusion, he said, 'I'm the commander of the Libération Normandie brigade,' and went back to his men. They took aim. One of the men who had

216

escorted the youngster was standing right next to me. I noticed the shadow of a rifle butt. It caught me behind the ear. The torch.

Everything was still. I moved my legs. My head felt as though it had been rammed down into my body. I lifted my shoulders. Day was dawning. I felt the back of my head. Clotted blood. I was lying not far from the manure pile.

The men were gone; the corpses had disappeared. Dark splashes on the whitewashed wall, pools on the ground. Near the straw, a bit of fabric from someone's clothes. I looked over the enclosure of the liquid manure pit. The farm was deserted, the fire burned out. It cost me an interminable effort to get to my feet. I shuffled over to the house, not thinking about my crutch. Unable to find a living soul, I sank down and leaned against the door frame. I was cold, and I didn't know what had become of my coat. After a few minutes, I stood up again and got out of there. A ringing in my ears accompanied every step. I tried to keep my head still.

Execution, I thought. They weren't Germans. A family feud? A name came to me: Libération Normandie. The man with the eyeglasses belonged to the Resistance. Like Chantal. I reached the farm gate, which hung askew, took my first step onto the dirt road, and heard the whimpering. There was the dog, dragging his chain in the dust. He ran back and forth, always to the end of the chain, barking as he ran, then snuffing and yapping; he wouldn't stop running. For a moment, I held on to the post. The dog was old, but I didn't trust him. I hobbled over to the lean-to, where the other end of his chain was fastened. Four bolts

217

driven through a metal plate. I couldn't loosen the chain. Then I noticed the mound. A rectangle of freshly shovelled earth. In the grass, not far away, a woman's jacket. The faces of the people lying under the mound appeared before me, farmers' faces in torchlight. The powerful father, the workers. The youngest son was no more than ten. I turned away.

When I walked over to the dog, he barked and backed up until he couldn't go any farther. I bent over. Hammering inside my skull. I reached for the dog's collar and unfastened the buckle. The chain fell to the ground. The dog stayed where he was. I straightened up slowly and didn't look at the fresh mound again. *Libération.* For the second time, I reached the gate. Pink stripes on the horizon; the little road led that way. I walked without a crutch, flapping an arm to maintain my balance. The dog stood at the gate. I hoped he'd come with me. He stayed where his people were buried. I heard him barking for a long time.

33

The farm faced south. The hill rose to the horizon, where a weathered bench under an ash tree promised a lovely view. The property had been described to me. I approached it with the sweeping gait I'd adopted since losing my crutch.

It was Sunday; no one in the fields. Some folks in their best outfits on the dusty road. The church apparently lay behind the hill. Although I knew the sea was many kilometres away, I kept waiting to see breakers from the top of the next rise or the one after that. I laughed. I felt afraid. I imagined walking with Chantal on the seashore, saw her naked feet in the sand. Not too fast, I said to myself. Be careful. You're going to fall. Slow down! I considered looking for something that might serve as a walking stick, because I didn't seem capable of holding myself back. I started going even faster, running up the hill, waving both arms around to stay upright. An elderly couple dressed in Sunday black turned around. I was ragged and unshaven, and by this time my leg splints were just two clattering pieces of wood. My jaw was healing badly, and my mouth always hung open a little. I wasn't worried about it. I laughed louder and ran so fast, my eyes got blurry. A bell rang somewhere. People were cresting the hill. I thought the Mass must be over.

I had imagined Chantal greeting me in a hundred different ways. Joyful, sleepy, effusive. Or unspeaking perhaps. Paris was months ago. I was sure she'd surprise me, as she always did.

I reached the farm. The door on the street side was locked. I assumed Chantal and her family would be coming back from Mass soon, and so I opted to wait. A dozen people passed, eyeing me curiously. I lost patience and walked around the stone house, whose western wall was covered with black slate. Behind the house, I came to an expanse of well-trodden ground, the centre of the farmstead. No grass; muddy puddles; a manure pit, enclosed and stinking. Four pigs in a ramshackle pigsty, lying idly in the sun. All at once, I saw myself as the tramp that I was. Would the family come back and run me off? I was relieved to see

219

there was no dog. The only sounds came from the pigs, snuffling in the slop.

The back door opened. An old woman looked out and disappeared again. On the floor above, a young girl's face appeared; when I noticed her, she stepped back from the window. Inside the house, the old woman spoke with someone who was deeply ensconced in the front room. I took a few cautious steps, holding my hands up and to the side to show that I was unarmed. When the door opened a second time, I heard a baby crying. Light from the other end of the hall, and inside the light an approaching shadow.

Old Joffo stepped into the farmyard. His hair was snow-white and blowing in the wind. The imposing boar had been transformed into a pallid, stooping creature. In spite of my disfigurement, he recognized me. We faced each other warily in the windy farmyard.

'From where?' he asked tonelessly.

'Paris.'

'Who knows you're here?' The wind blew his voice away.

'No one.' I stepped closer to him. His eyes fell on my splint.

'No one followed me,' I insisted.

The window on the upper floor went up. The young woman in the light blue overalls bore a distant resemblance to Chantal. Joffo noticed her.

After a little hesitation, he said, 'It's Roth.'

She jumped. Movement in the house. The old woman appeared in the hall. My name changed something, but it didn't elicit friendliness, only curiosity. The baby cried again. The young woman left the window. Joffo pointed indecisively toward a rain-bleached table that stood outside, near the house, on the only patch of green. I sat down, stretching out my leg with an effort; my uphill charge had done me in. Joffo took a seat on a stool across from me. The old woman remained at the back door. I was thirsty, but I said nothing. The young woman appeared on the ground floor, a bundle in her arm. The bundle was a baby, swaddled in linen. Only its dark hair was visible.

'And Chantal?' I could no longer hold the question back.

Joffo gazed at the child. I followed his eyes. 'Is she here?'

'No,' he said. 'She's not here anymore.'

I nearly collapsed from sheer disappointment. 'When do you expect her back?'

Joffo sat still; only his hair moved. I realized he didn't think she'd be back soon. Chantal wasn't in church or walking in the woods; Chantal was far away. I could feel it. Maybe fighting with another underground Resistance group, on the coast. So many weeks, such a long way! I'd been on an obstacle course. I'd reached Balleroy, but not my goal. I laid my hands on the table, one on top of the other.

'Would you take some food and drink?' a soft voice asked. The young woman placed the infant in the shade. She had bigger eyes than Chantal and dark hair. She walked like Chantal.

'Are you her sister?' I asked.

'Her cousin,' she said with a serious air.

'Your baby?' Now I could see the infant better. Black hair, wrinkled face, the eyes two sleeping slits.

The young woman didn't answer my question.

221

'How old?' I asked.

'Three weeks.'

'Will you stay for lunch?' Joffo asked.

'Yes, gladly.'

The woman went inside.

The grandmother sat on the bench that ran along the house wall and watched the young woman serve me. I ate bread and cream, along with a couple of carrots, and drank some tart old cider that cleared my head. I wasn't a guest in this house; I was a transient they were putting up with. They noticed how hard it was for me to chew. The left half of my jaw ground away uselessly. I gnawed the carrots like an old dog.

Joffo confirmed my fears. 'Where do you intend to go?'

'To Chantal.' It was the only answer. 'Where is she? I'll find her.'

The cousin took a step toward me as though she wanted to say something. Joffo silenced her with a gesture. He stood up and walked along the wall of the house. In the shade of a pear tree, there was a cellar door. He lifted it and disappeared inside. The old woman, the baby, the young woman, and I waited in silence. I bit off a piece of bread. Chantal's cousin filled my glass.

Joffo came back with a bottle of brandy. The old woman went inside and brought us two glasses. Joffo poured. The young woman sat on the ground beside the baby and shaded its face with her hand. Joffo glanced at the sun. At that moment, he was once again the narrow-eyed boar. We emptied our glasses.

The Germans had moved into Balleroy unexpectedly. A decimated company from the

222

south, on the way to Pas-de-Calais. They required food, drink, and lodging, and they commandeered quarters in three farmsteads.

'The captain was correct,' Joffo said. 'A man you could talk to. The men occupied the barns, and the officers came to the main house.'

He filled the glasses again and drank. I waited.

'Chantal and Jeanne gave up their room.' He moved his head in the cousin's direction. She was totally focused on the child.

'The two of them slept in the storeroom attached to the barn. We brought out our provisions; the women cooked them up. The soldiers didn't say much. They were on their way to the front. We thought—everyone in the village thought—it would be over in two days.'

A carrot had rolled off the table. Joffo picked it up and put it next to my plate. He drank a third glass of brandy. I stopped eating. A jackdaw shrieked somewhere nearby.

'The night before they moved out, one of the lieutenants discovered the cellar under the henhouse.' Joffo pointed to the south, where there were some young walnut trees misshapen by the wind. 'That was where we hid the things that weren't meant to be found.' He shrugged his shoulders. 'Supplies for a year. Weapons. The captain confiscated the weapons but forbade any looting. They all took their fill of the wine. Officers and men got drunk together.'

The old woman sat beside Joffo and looked past me, up the hill. He stayed quiet for a while.

'Later that night, the lieutenant went into the storeroom. Without paying attention to Jeanne, he pounced on Chantal. Jeanne came running out and woke me up. I grabbed a piece of firewood and ran out to the storeroom. When I got there, it was too late.'

Joffo ran his hand over his forehead.

'The lieutenant was dying, bleeding from many wounds. Chantal had pulled a dagger out of her belt and stabbed away. I told her to get away to some safe place. Chantal sat on the bloody bed and stared at the dagger. Then she tried to leave, but Jeanne's screaming had awoken the Germans.'

Joffo stood up and walked to the centre of the yard.

'The captain had his men bring her here,' he said. 'Right here.' He hung his head. 'We were all outside. The baby was asleep in my father's arms. My brother, the women, two workers. Chantal stood and faced the captain. It was cold that night. She was shivering. Without hesitating a second, without a single word, the captain pulled his pistol, pushed Chantal to the ground, and shot her in the back of the head.' Joffo's finger designated the spot.

He came back to the table. 'The shot woke up the baby, and it started crying.' He stopped in front of me and stared at the faded tabletop. The old woman remained seated, bolt upright.

'They put my brother against the wall, and also a worker who just happened to be at the farm that night. Then the soldiers came for my father. He gave Jeanne the baby, very carefully, and went and stood with the others. They were shot immediately.'

Joffo sat down and put one hand on top of the other. 'For every German killed, ten French citizens have to die,' he said. 'That's the ratio. But the captain was content with four. Dawn was already breaking. He ordered his men to move out. By sunrise, the company had left Balleroy. My father would have been eighty today.'

I caught myself doing the arithmetic. How many days, how many weeks? If I had set out earlier, if I had stuck to the main roads, if I had increased my daily distances . . .

Joffo went into the house and came out with the dagger. He laid it on the table.

'No one thought to take it.'

I hesitated. Then I drew the blade from the dark grey sheath. The blood had been washed off. I fixed my eyes on the steel.

'Was she buried?'

Instead of Joffo, the cousin answered. 'Do you want to see it?'

I ran my finger along the sharp blade. Clouds were gathering above the walnut trees. The wind died down all of a sudden. I had learned everything and understood nothing.

'What will you do?' I asked.

'Live on,' the bookseller said.

'We still have the child.' The old woman's eyes remained fixed on the hill.

I emptied my glass. The brandy was strong. I gazed at the little linen-swathed creature. 'What's its name?'

'Her name is Antoinette,' Joffo said.

I turned around. Slowly, I stood up; my splints knocked together. I hobbled over to the tree and bent down. The baby was asleep. She looked concerned, as though sleep required a lot of effort. I wanted to touch one of her little hands but didn't dare.

'Chantal's baby?' I asked. My knees trembled. Nobody spoke.

I stared at the tiny face. 'And the birth?'

'Easy,' the old woman said.

I thought of Chantal in the pale green dress, Chantal in rue Faillard. I looked directly at the sun and fell into whiteness. Stroked the little head. She flinched and made a face.

'Antoinette,' I said softly.

Later on, Jeanne made me a sleeping place in the barn. I sat on the blanket spread out on the hay. Flecks of sunlight played with motes of dust. I contemplated my hands, my missing finger, my splinted leg. Drawing the dagger out of the sheath for the second time, I set the point on my chest. I couldn't feel much through my jacket. I opened my shirt and pressed the dagger against my skin, watching it tighten and split open, watching the drop of blood spill out. I laid the dagger down beside me. All of a sudden, the hay smelled like Chantal's hair. I inhaled the scent, reaching for the dancing points of light. I screamed and clapped my hand over my mouth at the same time. I screamed into my hand. Saliva flowed into the folds of my palm. When dusk came on, I'd been staring out the window for hours. Chantal and Antoine. The time we escaped the raid. The time we kissed each other in Leibold's face. The time she was on top of me in rue Faillard. Her hair, her breasts. Never. Nothing.

That evening, I went to the main house and ate with the family. I sat there and chewed like the others. No lamps were lit. The spreading darkness united us. Afterward, I asked to see Antoinette. Jeanne led me into the storeroom. I took the baby

226

girl out of her cradle and held her against my chest. She didn't wake up. I squeezed her tightly. Her breath on my neck. She cried out. Jeanne reached to take her, but I held on to Antoinette and rocked her until she fell asleep again.

That night, I wanted to stay there. In Balleroy, close to the sea. I wanted to stay there; and the war was far away. Antoine and Antoinette. As I lay in the straw, I thought about the word *father.* I had no feeling for it.

The next day, they allowed me to carry Antoinette around. But when I headed out to the fields, they sent Jeanne after me. Later, I tried to help Joffo split firewood. He put the axe down without a word and went into the house.

They let me share their meals. They asked nothing and wanted to know nothing. They were hospitable to me, and yet they remained distant. I didn't talk about Paris or about my journey. I walked down the hill with the baby and Jeanne and asked her where the sea was. Too far, she replied, and anyway, you couldn't get there now. They were building bunkers and fences. Jeanne hadn't been to the beaches in a long time. We turned around. The baby was taken out of my arms and carried into the house.

'She's my child,' I said that night into the straw. 'They want to mourn without me, and they want to keep me away from my child.' Bewildered, I laughed into the rafter beams. 'I'm practically their son-in-law!'

The next day, I asked Jeanne to show me the grave. We took Antoinette with us. We had to go through the village to reach the cemetrey. No one was outdoors, but I knew there were people

227

watching me. I was the *boche*; they'd heard about me. In the second line of houses, there was one with its windows open. The radio was playing. The melody, carried on the wind, got louder and softer by turns. Someone was singing. I could understand very few words, but I recognized the tune. The singer was Chevalier, snappy and brazen: *'Avril prochain—je reviens.'* I started hobbling faster, trying to get closer to the house, but a fence barred my way. Carrying the baby in one arm, Jeanne followed me in amazement. By the time she caught up with me, the song was over.

The mounded earth was fresh. There was no gravestone, only a stone cross. A couple of flowers. I tried to kneel down, but my splint prevented me. Antoinette started to cry; the sun was strong. A heap of earth, with other graves around it. All that had nothing to do with Chantal. We turned back. It was unusually hot for the beginning of June. On the way back to the farm, I thought, You can't stay. They won't allow it.

I spent my days in the barn, presenting myself only to eat and to see the baby. One evening, I stayed after dinner and told the story of the executions in Heudebonville. Joffo shook his head.

'There's no brigade that calls itself Libération Normandie,' he said. 'There are just gangs. They see the Germans withdrawing from the interior and they take advantage of the situation.'

'They weren't bandits,' I answered. 'This was a planned operation.'

The old woman went outside. Jeanne bent over the baby in her lap.

'Then the farmer must have been a collaborator,' Joffo said. 'Reprisals are necessary.'

'Communists?' I asked.

He didn't answer.

The next day, he asked me to join him outside. Antoinette was lying in the shade.

Without a prologue, he said, 'When are you going to leave?'

I wanted to reply, but I didn't. I asked about the baby.

'How do you know you're the father?' he replied, stone-faced.

I just looked at him. 'Maybe, when all this is over . . .'

I fell silent.

'Antoinette is French. Her family is here,' the bookseller said. 'You can't take her away with you, and you can't stay here yourself. It's not possible.'

I looked at the hill. 'How far is it to the sea?'

He gazed at my leg. 'Too far for you.'

'I'd still like to see it.'

He wiped his forehead. 'Yes, fine,' he said in a friendlier voice. 'Tomorrow. Maybe tomorrow.'

The next day, I took Antoinette for one last walk in the fields.

I talked to her and told her about her mother. We fell asleep in the grass. She woke up agitated; her crying was smothered and soundless. I picked her up, stroked her back, and began to sing. About the girl I fell in love with, in the city, in April. I didn't know the right words, and soon I fell silent. Antoinette looked at me attentively. I told her I had to go now, and that it would be better for her to forget me. I said it for my own sake. Afterward, I gave the child back to Jeanne and received a bundle of provisions from the old woman and a pair of boots from Joffo. No more was said about the trip to the seashore.

I left in the grey light of dawn, no less an outsider than on the day I'd arrived. I took with me the dagger Chantal had used to defend herself. Many kilometres beyond Balleroy, ships were emerging from the early-morning fog; the first troops were landing, trying to gain a foothold. It was the sixth of June. I knew nothing about that. I was on the road.

AFTERWORD

Readers often ask me how the story of *April in Paris* originated and what sort of research I did into the historical background of the time.

The origin of my tale is quickly told. A few years ago, while hiking along a cliff on the Normandy coast, I realized I'd overestimated my strength and clambered out too far. I could neither advance nor retreat, and then it started to rain. Stuck on a ledge in the middle of a storm, I spotted the ruins of one of the German Wehrmacht's defensive bunkers on a tongue of land opposite me. And there on that ledge, I had the idea for *April in Paris*: the story of a young German soldier, all alone in a foreign land, striving to stay out of the conflicts of his day but unable to disengage himself from the inhumanity of the occupation regime. From that beginning, the entire constellation of an impossible love story developed.

For the portrayal of the historical background and the evocation of 'everyday life' in occupied Paris, I have drawn on many sources, from historical city maps to reference books and contemporary literary accounts. I'm particularly indebted to two authors and two books. The first is Arthur Koestler, whose work I greatly admire, and whose novel *Darkness at Noon*, first published in 1940, provided me with authoritative insight into prison conditions and interrogation methods in totalitarian countries. It was from Koestler's book that I first learned of the quadratic tapping alphabet, which my Corporal Roth also uses in his cell. The second author is Felix Hartlaub, a German soldier who was posted in Paris, among other places, during World War II. He died under murky circumstances in 1945, in the last days of the conflict. I learned a great deal about the soldiers' jargon of the time from his posthumously published book, *In den eigenen Umriss gebannt: Kriegsaufzeichnungen, literarische Fragmente und Briefe aus den Jahren 1939 bis 1945* (*In the Restricted Zone: Notes from the Second World War*), which was first published in 1955. Hartlaub was a rarity—an uncompromising and discerning witness. In a letter from Paris, he wrote about the atmosphere in the occupied city: 'The typical climate here is arctic. I see so many examples of progressive dehumanization, hair-raising egoism, and cold-blooded apathy that I constantly have to defend myself against invasions from these inner regions.' Perhaps Corporal Roth would have seen things in more or less the same way.

CHIVERS
LARGE
PRINT
–direct–

If you have enjoyed this Large Print book
and would like to build up your own
collection of Large Print books, please
contact

Chivers Large Print Direct

Chivers Large Print Direct offers you
a full service:

• Prompt mail order service

• Easy-to-read type

• The very best authors

• Special low prices

For further details either call
Customer Services on (01225) 336552
or write to us at Chivers Large Print Direct,
FREEPOST, Bath BA1 3ZZ

Telephone Orders:
FREEPHONE 08081 72 74 75